Childcraft

LIFE IN MANY LANDS

Childcraft

IN FOURTEEN VOLUMES

•

VOLUME FIVE

LIFE IN MANY LANDS

FIELD ENTERPRISES, INC.

CHICAGO

R.BUEHRIG

CHILDCRAFT
(Reg. U.S. Pat. Off.)

CONTENTS

[Alphabetical indexes of authors, titles, and first lines appear at the back of Volume Six.]

HOLIDAY STORIES

CHILDREN OF THE AMERICAS

STORIES OF MANY LANDS

5

ACKNOWLEDGMENTS

The publishers of CHILDCRAFT gratefully acknowledge the courtesy of the following publishers and authors for permission to use copyrighted stories, poems, and illustrations:

Child Life magazine and the authors for the following: "Eggs for Sale" by Alfred S. Campbell; "Jack-o-'Lantern" by Ruth Colby; "Indians for Thanksgiving" by Dorothy Heiderstadt; "Ringing in the New Year" by Cornelia Meigs; "Victor and the Pirate" by Ruby L. Radford; "Juan Brings a Valentine" by Lilith Sanford Rushing; "The Ghost of the Lagoon" by Armstrong Sperry.

Dodd, Mead & Company: "Sam Volney, Cowboy" from *A Cowhand Goes to Town* by Phil Stong, copyright 1939 by Phil Stong, courtesy Harold Matson.

Harper & Brothers: "The Sugar Snow" from *Little House in the Big Woods* by Laura Ingalls Wilder.

Houghton Mifflin Company: "Journey to America" from *Petar's Treasure* by Clara Ingram Judson; "Madelon Dances" from *Gay Madelon* by Ethel Calvert Phillips.

David McKay Company: "Christmas Eve on Beacon Hill" from *Benjy of Boston* by Frances Cavanah.

The Macmillan Company: "Nanette Visits the Château" from *Nanette of the Wooden Shoes* by Esther Brann; "Zebedee, Fisherman" from *Blue Teapot* by Alice Dalgliesh; "The Brothers One, Two, and Three" from *Traveling Shops* by Dorothy Rowe.

G. P. Putnam's Sons: "A Friend of Greece," adapted from *Wings for Nikias* by Josephine Blackstock, copyright 1942 by Josephine Blackstock, courtesy of Hutchinson & Co., Ltd., London.

Rinehart & Company, Inc.: "Hoosier Barbecue" by William E. Wilson, from *Thimble Summer* by Elizabeth Enright, copyright 1938 by Elizabeth Enright Gillham; "Locked In" from *Picnic Adventures*, edited by Elizabeth L. Gilman, copyright 1940 by Rinehart & Company, Inc.

Ruge, Louise E. Baldwin: "Silver Pesos for Carlos" from *The American Junior Red Cross News*.

Simmonds, Martha F.: "Young Mountainy Singer" from *What To Do*, courtesy of David C. Cook Publishing Company.

Simon, Charlie May: "Christmas in the Piney Woods" from *Story Parade*.

Story Parade, Inc.: "In Honor of a Gaucho" by Katherine Pollack, copyright 1947 by Story Parade, Inc.

Viking Press, Inc.: "Bluebonnets for Lucinda" from *Bluebonnets for Lucinda* by Frances Clarke Sayers, copyright 1934 by Frances Clarke Sayers and Helen Sewell; "The Tramp" from *Tidewater Tales* by Anne Littlefield Locklin, copyright 1942 by Anne Littlefield Locklin; "Star-Spangled Banner Girl" from *Children of the Handcrafts* by Carolyn Sherwin Bailey, copyright 1935 by Carolyn Sherwin Bailey; "The Fair" from *The Good Master* by Kate Seredy, copyright 1935 by Kate Seredy.

Zobarskas, Stepas: "Music of the Scythes" from *The American Junior Red Cross News*.

HOLIDAYS AND FESTIVALS

MARY MILLER

Ringing in the New Year

By Cornelia Meigs

FRANKLIN STREET was so empty that Julia Stone was singing to herself as she walked along through the snow. She did not sing very well, and so it was only when there was nobody near by to hear that she lifted up her voice and hummed a little song. Nobody else was moving down the street of the little New Hampshire village, where the thin veil of snow was falling everywhere. In every house, however, there was a glow of warm fires behind the windows and a bright holly wreath left over from Christmas hanging between the curtains. Above her, she could just barely see the tall spire of the church against the gray sky, with the cloud of falling snow wrapping it all around.

For Judy it was going to be a very special New Year indeed. Her mother had said that when she was eleven, she could sit up until midnight to see the old year out. Nancy Hyde, her best friend, had been told the same thing by her mother. And this year they were both eleven, although with Judy there was only one week to spare. She was going to sit up at Nancy's house and spend the night there. Yes, this was to be a new and exciting New Year's Eve.

The telephone rang just as she came into the house. Her mother and father had gone to see some friends in the next town

8

ten miles away. Judy ran to answer and heard her mother's voice sounding faint and far away, for the telephone was not working very well.

"Judy, can you hear me? We'll have to spend the night with our friends. The road through Lyme Hollow will be drifted so deep we ought not to try it when it is getting dark. Anna will see that you have your supper and get safely over to Nancy's. But I'm worried about one thing. You know your father and I always go on the last day of the year to see Mr. Townly and take him a load of firewood. Simon Hammonds was to bring it this afternoon. But the snow—"

The telephone sputtered and then gave no sound. The storm was interfering with it. Then suddenly it began to be clear again.

"Judy—Judy, are you still there? I'm afraid Simon can't get into town with his little truck. I know Mr. Townly will be out of wood because he expects ours. Ask Nancy's father if he won't send one of his trucks and see that Mr. Townly gets it somehow—"

Once more the telephone broke off. At last Central spoke. "I can't get the connection any more. The weight of the snow has brought down a wire or a pole somewhere."

Judy put down the receiver. Yes, of course, someone had to see that Mr. Townly got his wood. Mr. Townly was the pleasant old man who made the fires in the church and swept the Sunday-school rooms and always had such a kind word for every boy or girl in town. It was he who rang the bell in the tall spire of the church, rang it mornings and evenings, for Sunday services and for particular occasions. Mr. Townly was poor, and his little house at the end of the street could be very cold. Judy knew that on a winter night a low woodpile was a serious matter even in her own household.

In houses like Mr. Townly's there were no furnaces. In bitter weather someone often had to be up until morning to keep fires in stoves and fireplaces from going out. If you had nothing to burn, you could not just telephone a dealer down the street and have him bring a load of coal or wood. No, you had to send word to Mr. Hammonds, and he had to fetch it over three miles of bumpy road—if his truck would run. In this snow it probably would not.

Judy turned and ran out of the house. She was breathless when she got to Nancy's house, three blocks beyond the church. Nancy ran to take her wet coat, but Judy could not stop except to get her breath. She explained about Mr. Townly's wood, but Nancy's father had driven out to the power plant and her mother was out and would not be back until evening.

But Nancy's Cousin Martha Hand was sitting by the fire knitting. She went to college and was here for the Christmas vacation. Nancy's brother Tom had just come in and was still in his big boots and heavy jacket. He had been shoveling snow at the kitchen door.

Cousin Martha put down her knitting to listen, and Tom

stopped beating his snowy mittens against the fender. "That's bad," Tom said. "Of course, Hammonds can't get in with the wood. Poor old Mr. Townly!"

Everyone was fond of Mr. Townly. His father and his grandfather had rung the church bell before him. Every man, woman, and child in the town got up by him, started to school by him, went to church in the quiet of Sunday morning to his ringing. He and those who had rung before him had never missed a morning or a church service or a public festival. Everybody knew that Mr. Townly had to be taken care of. And now all the older people were out of reach and these younger ones must do it. But how?

"There's the big truck out in the barn," Tom said. "Father had it brought in last night from the plant. That could get out to the Hammonds place, but who's to drive it? I know how, but I haven't got my license yet." Tom was fifteen, and the law would

not let him drive for another year. Cousin Martha jumped.

"I could drive it. I drove a truck when I was visiting on the farm last summer. But how will we get the wood loaded if Mr. Hammonds isn't there?"

"Oh, we can get plenty of people, like Jim Stevens and Polly and the others. If there are enough of us we can get it on all right. We'll pick them up as we go down the street."

They were off in no time at all. Martha, in her bright ski suit, climbed to the high seat and shifted the big gears. The truck groaned and creaked and began to creep backward out of the shed. Martha backed it round neatly and came out onto the road. The drifts were getting deeper, but the truck went ploughing steadily along. They stopped at one house after another and explained the situation. Warmly clad boys and girls climbed aboard at each stop.

Three miles is a long way in the snow, but they got to Mr. Hammonds' house at last. He threw open the door when they chugged into his yard and came running out. "There now, I'm glad you came," he said. "I could never get into town myself with my small truck. I couldn't even get the wood loaded, for I'm trying to dig out a path to the stable and the sheep shed before the snow gets too much for me. The wood is piled back of the big barn. If each of you takes a stick at a time, you can get it loaded all right. It's lucky there are so many of you. But do you know how to take down a woodpile and load it in the truck? It has to be done right."

They all were sure that they could load the wood. Six of the boys and girls, Nancy and Judy among them, stood knee-deep in the snow and handed up the cut sticks, one at a time, to the other six in the truck. How they worked!

"We're all so plastered with snow, you'd think we had been having a snowball fight," Martha said. "Climb on and hold tight.

RINGING IN THE NEW YEAR

There will be plenty of bumps going home."

It was dark as they rumbled back to town, with the long fingers of the headlights feeling out the way ahead. The windows of all the houses were bright behind the holly wreaths as they rolled down Franklin Street. "Now run home to your suppers," Martha said, "and come back when we take the wood to Mr. Townly. It will have to be unloaded and piled up in his shed to do him any good."

It was quite late before they were all together again. People kept sending word. "Don't go without Jane, or Fred." "I have a package of cookies," or "Mr. Smith's overcoat that he isn't wearing." Anna and Martha were sewing up a flannel jacket for Mrs. Townly. It was really as late as everybody's bedtime when they were ready to start out again. But it was New Year's Eve tonight, and nobody's bedtime really mattered.

Judy thought she had never seen Mr. Townly's house look so small or so cold as it did that night. There must be only one light and one fire in it, and two people sitting close together, wondering how they could get through that bitter night.

What fun it was to shout, when the door opened, "Hello Mr. Townly, hello Mrs. Townly," to see their surprised faces, to put wood on the fireplace, to feed the cold stove in the kitchen until it roared. While some of the company stayed outside with Tom to pile the wood up in the shed, the others ran back and forth carrying in the boxes and bundles that had been sent. Martha had brought a can of milk and some packages in a basket, and she opened them in the kitchen. When all of them were gathered in the house at last, there was hot cocoa to hand around and there were plates piled up with cookies. They all sat down in front of the fire, most of them on the floor. Then Mr. Townly told them about when he was the age of Tom and went away to sea because the little New Hampshire town "seemed a sight too small for me."

He had had many adventures everywhere in the world. "But I came back in the end," he said. "When my father could not ring the church bell any more, I came back, first to help him, and then to keep on ringing it after he was gone. My son will do the same thing. He's out West now, driving cattle on that big ranch in Montana that belongs to Tom's uncle. But he'll come home, too. There are some jobs that are for the young and some for those who are growing older. This is a good town to come home to."

He looked at the big clock ticking on the wall. "Time's getting on. I can't be late ringing the church bell to bring the New Year in." He hurried into his worn old overcoat.

Tom had been out to look at the weather and came in stamping the snow off his boots. "The drifts are deep, Mr. Townly," he said. "We can't hope to drive the truck home tonight."

14

RINGING IN THE NEW YEAR

"Mr. Townly," asked Martha, "would it be so terrible if just this one year the bell didn't ring for New Year's Eve?"

"Why, such a thing has never happened," he answered. "Do you know that bell rang when the news came that the Declaration of Independence was signed in Philadelphia? It rang when George Washington was made President, it rang when Abraham Lincoln died, it rang for peace at the end of the last war. This has been a hard year, and there's many who will listen for it. If they don't hear it, they will think bad luck has come to the town for certain. They'll begin the New Year with heavy hearts and no courage. Oh, it has to ring!"

In spite of all they could say, he started out. Amongst them, they managed to help him through the big drift at the gate, but when they got out into the road the way was even harder. He struggled on for a few yards, then stopped, and swayed. He would have fallen if Tom had not caught him.

Somehow they got the old man back to his home and into a big chair before the fire. Anxiously they clustered round, rubbing his hands, and helping Mrs. Townly to cover him with warm blankets. No one noticed the time until Mr. Townly said, feebly, "The bell! It must ring!"

The children looked at one another in dismay. It was a quarter of twelve!

"We'll ring it for you," Julia said. "We'll ring it on time."

The children seconded her eagerly. In a moment, warmly wrapped, they were out of the house and on their way. The snow had stopped falling, but it lay so deep and smooth everywhere that it was hard to know places and corners and fenceposts that marked the way. The clouds had broken and the stars were out, very small and high in the cold air. Silently they pushed and fought their way through the deep snow, the older ones helping the little ones.

As they came nearer to the middle of the town, they found that some of the walks had been cleared and they could make more haste. Out of a few houses came the sound of voices, where there were parties going on. Then even these sounds ended, for it was nearly midnight and everyone was listening for the bell. The little town with its small, beautiful old houses, its broad street in the starlight, its yellow lights behind little window-panes—we must not fail it, Judy thought. They could see the church spire, going up above them against the stars. Now they had reached it. They were on time.

Tom had Mr. Townly's lantern and watch and the big key. Inside, the church was very black and little warmer than was the clean, crisp air outdoors. The light of the lantern showed the narrow door and the steps going up, up into the dark. Tom went first, carrying the lantern. Martha came last with a tiny

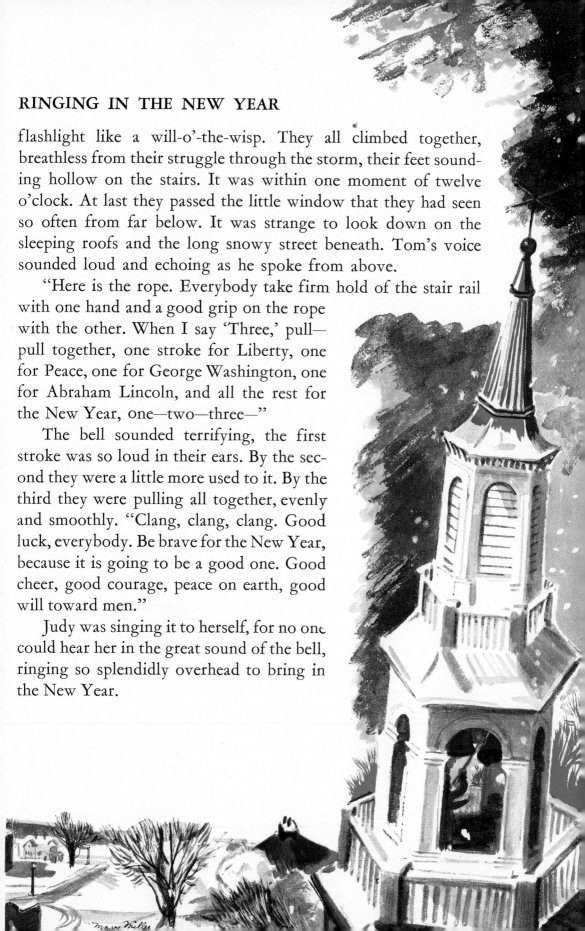

RINGING IN THE NEW YEAR

flashlight like a will-o'-the-wisp. They all climbed together, breathless from their struggle through the storm, their feet sounding hollow on the stairs. It was within one moment of twelve o'clock. At last they passed the little window that they had seen so often from far below. It was strange to look down on the sleeping roofs and the long snowy street beneath. Tom's voice sounded loud and echoing as he spoke from above.

"Here is the rope. Everybody take firm hold of the stair rail with one hand and a good grip on the rope with the other. When I say 'Three,' pull— pull together, one stroke for Liberty, one for Peace, one for George Washington, one for Abraham Lincoln, and all the rest for the New Year, one—two—three—"

The bell sounded terrifying, the first stroke was so loud in their ears. By the second they were a little more used to it. By the third they were pulling all together, evenly and smoothly. "Clang, clang, clang. Good luck, everybody. Be brave for the New Year, because it is going to be a good one. Good cheer, good courage, peace on earth, good will toward men."

Judy was singing it to herself, for no one could hear her in the great sound of the bell, ringing so splendidly overhead to bring in the New Year.

Juan Brings a Valentine

By Lilith Sanford Rushing

JUAN paused in his rapid walking and looked wistfully across the brownish-orange hills. He wished the day would come when he would not have to hurry so. It filled his throat with a sort of choky something to look across the beautiful row of hills. They rose so high that the sky seemed to rest peacefully on them.

He delighted in reaching the highest bronze hill and in looking far below where lay the great Wharton sheep ranch. His father, Pedro Santos, worked on the ranch. A half mile away, clustered in some scrubby trees, Juan could see his home where he lived with his father and mother and small sister, Anita.

Behind him lay a twisted trail that led to the road. This road had taken him to a new world. Here he hastened every morning to catch the bus that took him to the school where the white children went. Once it had frightened him terribly—this road, this bus, this school, and the children who had stared at him that first morning. But after days of loneliness, Juan, ten-year-old Mexican Indian boy, had found that the white children meant to be kind. The teacher, with her smiling eyes and soft hands, wanted him to become a good American. And now the desire burned like a flame —to become a child of this wonderful new country and speak its language.

This afternoon, Juan, his small brown face serious, was saying over and over, "Valentine! Valentine's Day! What a beautiful word valentine is! It sounds just as the sky looks!"

Miss Hawkins, the teacher, had patiently explained to Juan

18

JUAN BRINGS A VALENTINE

about St. Valentine's Day.

"We're to have a valentine box," she said. "We'll draw names, and everyone will give someone else a valentine."

Juan had drawn Jerry Cole's name, and he was in despair. He remembered that the valentines in the little store near the school cost money, and he scarcely knew what money looked like. Pedro, his father, seldom had any. When he wanted beans or meal, he went to the ranch house, and received what he needed in exchange for his work.

The boy brushed at some stray tears, then hurried over the hills toward the Wharton sheep ranch. He must hurry home and work. He must bring in water and carry in brush for the fires. Some days he had to help his father with the sheep.

That evening at supper Juan did not mention St. Valentine's Day. Usually he told his parents everything about school and his new friends. Their faces would grow bright, and not a word would they speak until he had finished. But tonight Pedro looked worried. Juan sat silently eating his cold beans and bread, and did not say a word.

After a while Pedro spoke to his wife in Spanish. "The last shipment of wool did not pay the expense. I got no money."

Juan's heart sank. How could he bear to go to school on St. Valentine's and have nothing to put in the box!

The next day and the next the children at school talked of little else except the valentines.

"I'm going to put in a big one, with a pink lacy frill around the edge," said one girl.

"Mine will be as large as a plate, and will have silver stars," said a boy.

Juan slipped about the corner of the school. He was afraid some one would ask him what kind he was going to bring.

Two days before Valentine's, Juan walked over the hills slowly

toward his home. His heart was so heavy he did not see the beauty about him. His father opened the door.

"My son, I've been waiting long hours for you," he cried. "Why have you fooled your time away playing on the trail? Old Jesu is sick, and you must go look after his sheep until another herder comes. Go up in the north hills at once, and when you pass Jesu's cottage don't take any money. One does not take pay when one labors for the sick."

So Juan turned and started up the rocky path to the hills. The good dog, Shep, trotted at his heels and brushed his nose against his hand. Juan talked to Shep in Spanish, for he feared the dog could not understand American words. Shep was a splendid old dog and had worked with sheep a long time. Juan was confident that they could look after Jesu's sheep.

The sheepherding was not a difficult task, and when the shadows were long on the mountain trail Juan and Shep found their way home. They passed by Jesu's cottage, and he took a coin and offered it to Juan. But Juan, shaking his head, hurried away, saying to himself, "One doesn't take money when one labors for the sick." Juan caught the great warm ear of Shep, and together they trotted down the rocky trail.

The day before Valentine's Juan got a peep at some valentines the other children had brought. Some one would put a valentine in the box for him. But Jerry would get no valentine, he thought sadly. Juan decided to ask his mother if he might stay at home the

JUAN BRINGS A VALENTINE

next day. He would rather not go without a Valentine.

But this evening he must go again to look after old Jesu's sheep, and he hurried away with Shep by his side.

The sheep were farther away than usual. Juan and Shep finally found them between two sloping hills. Near by the timber began. Cedars and oaks dotted the hillside. Juan paused with Shep. His school life with the white children seemed far away now, but still his heart ached with disappointment.

"They'll never ask me to do things with them again," he said aloud.

He sat on a rock for several minutes, trying to keep back the tears. Suddenly Shep gave a fierce bark and sprang forward with teeth showing. Juan jumped up like a flash. A great gray timber wolf had come from the trees and was attacking a lamb. When the wolf saw Shep coming, it turned to meet him and to fight. Juan picked up a heavy stick. He rushed to the spot where the wolf and dog were springing for each other's throats. The wolf made one leap, but was stopped by Shep.

Shep's teeth closed on the wolf's shoulder, but Juan saw, with a sinking heart, that the wolf's teeth had gone into Shep's neck dangerously near the throat. Locked together, the two animals rolled over and over. The panic-stricken sheep were running hither and thither.

Juan, stepping closer, watched his chance. He raised the heavy stick to strike. But how could he hit the wolf and not Shep? He must strike soon, for

the wolf had his teeth in poor Shep's throat. Juan, with all his strength, brought the stick down. Luckily it was the wolf's head he managed to hit. This gave the wolf a surprise, so Juan struck again and again. Shep did the rest, and soon the battle was over. The wolf was dead, and Shep was not badly injured.

When Juan and Shep reached home, Pedro was waiting for them. "Juan, why are you so late?" he asked.

Juan showed him the fresh skin of the timber wolf which he had been carrying slung over an arm.

"Uh, a timber wolf; a big one too! You're a brave boy and Shep is a brave dog. You may sell the skin, my boy, and take the money for yourself," cried Pedro proudly.

That night as Juan crawled beneath his blanket he was very happy. A wonderful plan had come to him. The next morning he started to school early, and was hurrying along happily when he was stopped by a peculiar sound. Looking about, he saw old Shep coming toward him with a baby wolf in his mouth.

Juan's eyes opened in surprise. The wolf he and Shep had killed had left a baby! He took the little shaking animal up in his arms and let it nestle against his coat.

"What can I do with this at school all day?" he thought. As there seemed no answer to this question, he wrapped the baby more securely in his coat and hurried on.

He reached the school store first. The storekeeper had his two windows and his counters spread with gorgeous valentines. Juan had never seen such beautiful ones! He stopped to gaze at them, overcome with awe at their beauty.

"My! My!" cried the storekeeper, coming up. "What do you have here? A baby wolf! Isn't he a little beauty!"

But Juan was intent on the valentines. Now perhaps he could buy one for the box. "Señor, would you let me have a valentine in exchange for this wolfskin?" he asked.

JUAN BRINGS A VALENTINE

"Why, I'd let you have a whole box of them for that skin, and two dollars besides," was the man's reply.

"Then I'll have a box of valentines to give Jerry Cole," cried Juan in delight.

"Yes, and I'll put the baby wolf in a box so you can carry him easily," said the storekeeper.

So Juan waited while the man got down a box of valentines, and watched him place the baby wolf in a similar box. The boy had never been so happy as he was when he hurried away, carrying the two boxes. He only wished the baby wolf was at home where his mother could give it some warm goat's milk. But it snuggled down in the box and lay quiet as if it wanted to sleep.

The schoolyard was buzzing with excitement when Juan came up. The children looked at his two boxes with wide eyes. Just then the bell rang and they marched into the big, pleasant schoolroom and took their seats. Juan placed his two boxes under his desk. The baby wolf, sleeping quietly, did not whimper. The teacher, passing Juan, smoothed his shiny black hair with her soft fingers. Juan was too happy to speak.

The valentine box would be the first on the program. A boy went about collecting the valentines. Juan handed him one of his boxes on which he had written: "For Jerry Cole."

Everyone stared at Juan's box but no one said a word. Juan sat up, proud and straight, when the valentines were being given away. Little girls rushed about delivering them when the names were called.

"Juan Santos," called Miss Hawkins, and a girl with a big pink bow on her yellow curls brought Juan's valentine to him.

He held it in his hands tenderly. His first valentine! He took it from its white envelope, his heart beating hard. It was all bright and red with a picture in the center, and at the top there was a real bow of silk ribbon.

JUAN BRINGS A VALENTINE

The box for Jerry Cole was called last. Every one was looking at Jerry when he opened it. There was a moment of silence, and Jerry's eyes opened wide. Then he gave a shriek of joy. From the box he drew a tiny, quivering baby wolf, with bright inquisitive eyes and a furry coat.

"Oh look what I got!" Jerry cried. "Just look at my valentine! Mine can breathe and see and move! I've got the dandiest valentine in the whole world!"

The children arose in their seats and began clamoring for a sight of Jerry's valentine. Miss Hawkins came to Jerry's side and stroked the baby wolf's soft furry coat.

"From Juan Santos," she said aloud and all eyes were turned toward Juan.

And Juan saw in those eyes respect and honor for him and his present. He was so surprised he could not speak. The boxes had gotten mixed and Jerry had the one containing the baby wolf. But it was all right. He would take the box of valentines home for his mother and little Anita.

Then Jerry turned to him crying, "Oh, Juan, thanks! But what is his name?"

Juan looked up. "His name is Valentine," he said.

The Tramp

A Story of Virginia

By Anne Littlefield Locklin

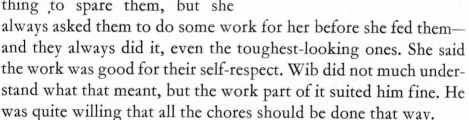

WHEN Grandfather Wib was a boy, tramps often came to the back door to ask for a bite to eat. There was a railroad junction a mile north, and the tramps followed along the tracks and stopped for food at houses on the way. Wib's mother never seemed to be the least bit afraid of any of the tramps. She always found something to spare them, but she always asked them to do some work for her before she fed them— and they always did it, even the toughest-looking ones. She said the work was good for their self-respect. Wib did not much understand what that meant, but the work part of it suited him fine. He was quite willing that all the chores should be done that way.

One day, toward the end of March, Cousin Ned and Wib and Shorty had an argument on the way home from school.

It seemed that one of the older boys, Lank Smith, had said that tramps who stop at your house have a way of leaving signs behind them so that all the tramps who come along will know whether your house is a good one to stop at.

"Do you believe that?" Ned wanted to know.

Shorty said, "It must be so. Why, old Missus Peele boasts that no tramp has entered her gate in twenty years. She's **too** stingy to give away a bread crust, and I bet anything the tramps all know it beforehand."

Wib said he didn't believe it, and he wanted to know what the signs looked like. "I've never seen a tramp make any marks around our house, and you know how many stop there," he said. "I'm glad of it. Why, every now and then I don't have a stick of kindling to split and I remember once I got out of dipping water from the rain barrel and lugging it into the house on washday," he boasted. "I like tramps."

"Huh," Shorty said, and he kicked at a hunk of melting snow with his boots and sent it flying in a fine spray. "Liking 'em doesn't prove anything. We were talking about signs."

"Oh, well," Ned said, "don't get het up about it. The old tramps will be coming back pretty soon and then we'll see who is right." Most of the tramps in that region were like the robins—they went south in the winter and came back in the spring. "Let's cut across lots and see if the pussy willows are out," he added.

Then the boys followed the brook down through the orchard to the footbridge. Wib was proud to see that the bridge still held despite the high water. The snow had pretty well gone off in the open, except for places where drifts had been—the brook would not get much higher. They crossed, stopped for a drink all around at the spring, then sloshed up the path to the house. A delicious aroma of hot molasses and spice came through the open kitchen window.

"Cookies," Ned said. "Aunt Annie is at it again." They made a rush for the back door. But they stopped long enough in the back room to take off their caps and to wipe their feet—they were well trained that way.

All the boys thought that Wib's mother made the best things to eat. There were doughnuts and pies to make your mouth water. But cookies were her specialty—and she could make every kind you ever heard of. Molasses cookies, sugar cookies, hermits, ginger puffs, and raisin cookies—the big brown crock was never empty.

THE TRAMP

Now as the boys unwound their mufflers and unbuttoned their overcoats, she took a great pan of golden brown cookies from the oven. "I don't blame the tramps for stopping at your house," Shorty said, as he watched her.

Mother Annie smiled and her blue-gray eyes twinkled. "Do you remember last year when I gave a tramp some molasses cookies?"

Wib and Ned knew the story, but Shorty had not heard it. So Wib's mother told it again. First she put two sticks of wood in the stove and fixed the draft. Then she began. "About this time last spring, a big burly old tramp stopped to ask if I could spare him a bite to eat. I told him if he would fetch a pail of water from the spring I would see. And while he was getting the water, I fixed him a big plate of cookies. It so happened it was April first and I had been making some molasses cookies about like these, only I put cotton batting inside one or two of them to fool the boys." Wib and Ned grinned—they remembered those cookies.

"Of course the cotton didn't show, once they were baked," she went on, "and somehow I got hold of one of those April Fool cookies and put it on the plate with the others. You should have seen the surprised look on that big fellow's face when he bit into the cotton. I couldn't help laughing."

"And what did the tramp do?" Shorty wanted to know.

"Oh, he laughed too," Mother Annie said. "Laughed until I thought he'd burst the last button on his coat."

It made the boys laugh just to think of it and Mother Annie joined in. She was like that. She always loved a joke.

Now she gave them a plateful of hot cookies and a couple of Russet apples apiece and they went out to eat by the back door where the wind didn't hit and the last bit of sun did. It was nice and warm out there on the flat stone that served as a doorstep. There was silence for a full minute while the boys crunched and munched.

THE TRAMP

The afternoon shadows were purple-black, but the sun had that peculiar yellow brilliance that spring sunshine seems to have about that time of day. It searched out the patch on Wib's short trousers where he had torn them on the picket fence, and the darns on the knees of Ned's black stockings now faded a greenish hue, and the tiny mended moth holes in Shorty's gray coat. Wib began to shine one of the Russets on his trousers. Russets are a bronzy apple speckled all over like Shorty's nose in midsummer. They're the best keepers of all the New Hampshire apples, but they never take a very high shine.

"I've been thinking," Shorty said. "What if that big old tramp had got mad at your mother?"

"Huh," Wib said. "She's not afraid of tramps!" and he bit a wormhole out of his apple and spit it out scournfully.

"I know—my mother says the usual tramp is perfectly harmless," Ned put in. "But what I'd like to know is how you going to tell which is which?"

Wib stood up. "Pooh! No tramp ever hurt a flea," he said, "I'd just like to see one that could scare me!" And he puffed out his chest like a young Tom turkey when he said it.

All this time Mother Annie was in the pantry cutting out more cookies. She had the window open a crack and she stood

28

before it working. When Wib looked up and saw her smiling and her eyes twinkling, he didn't think anything of it, only how pretty she looked standing there with her almost black hair combed back smoothly from her forehead and her cheeks all rosy from baking —sort of like a picture in a frame. He didn't mind that there was a smootch of flour over one eyebrow.

There wasn't much more time for their arguing. All three of the boys had chores to do before supper and the sun was dropping fast. Wib knew with all that baking his mother had done the kitchen wood box would take a sight of wood, and he set to work to fill it.

A few days later when Wib came home from school and ran in to get a bite to eat, he found a tramp sitting in the middle of the kitchen warming himself at the stove. He didn't think it strange to see a tramp there. Tramps always came with the spring, but it was strange that his mother was nowhere about. Perhaps she was upstairs getting something of his father's for the tramp to wear—he was certainly ragged enough—and all slumped down as if he were worn out. So he called, "Mother," loudly. There was no answer.

The tramp did not speak, but he raised his head and looked at Wib. Wib did not feel nearly so sure about tramps as he had been a few days before. This was the roughest-looking tramp Wib had seen in a long time. He had black bushy whiskers, and fierce black eyebrows, and his hat was jammed down over one eye. And when he looked at Wib with his one visible eye, a chill chased down Wib's spine. He was just ready to back out of the kitchen and shut the door after him. Then he thought, "No, I just can't run out and leave a tramp in the house and nobody home." A good deal was expected of a boy going on nine years.

So he screwed up his courage and tried to make his voice sound very big. "What are you doing in my mother's kitchen, sir?" The tramp didn't even look up this time.

"I'm hungry," he said, and his voice sounded awfully gruff.

Wib said, "My mother always asks the men who come for food," and he was very careful to be polite and not say tramps, "to do some work for her before she feeds them." The old fellow shook his head. "My mother says that's only just," Wib urged, hoping that the tramp would play fair. But the tramp just sat huddled down in his chair.

"Got rheumatism," he grunted, and still didn't look up.

Just then Wib remembered he had left his bank on the kitchen table. He could not see whether it was still there, for his mother had set her tins of bread dough on the table to rise, and had covered them over with a big cloth. He wanted desperately to go and look under the cloth. There was a lot of money in that bank—

THE TRAMP

boat money it was. Ever since fall when old Breshnahan had told them about his boat, Wib had been saving for one of his own. It came to ninety-three cents when he had counted it out at noon. He remembered that Ned's mother said that the usual tramp was perfectly honest, but he was quite sure that this was not a usual tramp.

What was Wib to do? He wanted to be rid of the fellow. He thought the tramp would go as soon as he was fed, and he knew where there was plenty of bread and butter and cookies. Yet he felt he should stick to the rule his mother always followed about working first. He would try once more and be extra polite. "I'm sorry about the rheumatism," Wib said, "and I'm sure Mother would be. If you would fetch just one small pail of water from the spring, I'm sure she wouldn't mind if I gave you something to eat."

"Good for you, Wibbie," the tramp said. And before Wib could move in his tracks, the tramp pulled off his hat, jerked off his whiskers and eyebrows and there sat his mother. "April Fool," she said and began to laugh. Of course, it was April first. Wib had forgotten for the moment. He ran and hugged her and they both laughed and laughed until they cried.

From *Tidewater Tales*

31

Ora Walker

Star-Spangled Banner Girl

A True Story for Flag Day and the Fourth of July

By Carolyn Sherwin Bailey

CAROLINE Pickersgill had learned to sew as soon as she could hold a needle. While her mother kept their little red brick house in old Baltimore spotless and shining, Caroline sat beside her grandmother Rebecca and stitched—first the long seams of handwoven sheeting, so long and stiff for little fingers to hold; then a calico dress for her wooden doll. That was fun! After that, she embroidered scallops for pantalets and petticoats, and matched the countless tiny squares of colored cloth that made the pattern of patchwork quilts. Caroline could hardly have been patient enough to sit sewing, quiet and industrious, in her small red rocking chair, if old Rebecca, her grandmother, had not told her stories to shorten the work. They were thrilling stories, for Rebecca Young had made a flag for General Washington to carry when the American Army took part in the siege of Boston.

The story always began with Rebecca's description of her Philadelphia flag shop. Then Caroline's grandmother Rebecca would go on to tell of the visit of General Washington to her shop, of his order for a flag which should have thirteen stripes of red and white, one for each of the colonies. In the corner of this flag was a "grand union" of the old British flag, a blue field with the red and white crosses of St. Andrew and St. George.

Soon after this flag was delivered to General Washington, Rebecca had been obliged to flee with her children in an oxcart going West. Her silver spoons and the Bible had been lost in the forest. There had been her struggle in the wilderness of western Pennsylvania, and then their return to this pleasant home in Baltimore. The entire countryside remembered how Rebecca had made General Washington's battle flag. Beautiful needlework was their family pride, Rebecca told Caroline. Her own fingers were too stiff now to make the tiny stitches for which the family was celebrated. But Caroline's mother, Mary Pickersgill, who had been only a baby when they fled from Philadelphia, still made flags occasionally. Perhaps some day Caroline also would stitch well enough to sew together stripes of red and white bunting, her grandmother said.

Peace and happiness filled the house where these three, Rebecca, Mary, and Caroline, lived alone. Caroline's father was dead, but they owned their brick house near the water front in Baltimore. Mary made a fair living for them, stitching more and more of the banners that Caroline watched going out toward the sea, flying above the merchant ships and sailing vessels. The American Revolution was nothing but history to the little girl. Now another war was going on—the War of 1812. It was hard to believe, however, when the bees hummed drowsily in their garden and the hens clucked

contentedly over their nests.

But Carolyn often wondered at what she saw from the Baltimore wharf. She loved to go down to the wharf, just a step from their front gate. She liked to follow with her eyes the crimson trail her mother's flags made as the ships bearing them put out to sea from Chesapeake Bay. For almost two years many of these flags had been pulled down before they were out of sight. Seamen had been taken from the American ships by British cruisers, and sometimes the ships themselves had been impressed into British service after they were captured.

Still this War of 1812 meant very little to Caroline Pickersgill. It was now two years since her mother's banners had first been torn from ships' rigging, and the small town of Baltimore still dozed beneath its white church steeples, its elm trees and flowering hedges. Caroline had come to think that the British and American ships were playing a game out there at sea, and this game was helping give her mother more work. Mary Pickersgill made a new flag for every one torn down, and Grandmother Rebecca folded each one carefully, sending it to sea with her blessing.

It was August of the year 1814. Caroline had never been so happy. She was a tall girl now, with a flowered bonnet, and with dainty dimity and muslin dresses billowing about her silk slippers. She was fourteen years old, and she could sew better than any of her friends. She made all her own clothes, from her embroidered chemises to the lace mitts that reached from her slender wrists to the edge of her puffed sleeves.

Sewing was not Caroline's only hand skill either. Her mother spent all her time in their flag shop, too busy to do the housework. Rebecca was seventy-five years old, and growing blind. She sat in the garden all summer long, trying to see the colors on the ships as they sailed out; and in the winter she huddled by the fireplace, telling over again the story of General Washington's visit. Caroline did the family sewing, baked bread, tended the garden, kept the pewter plates and the silver spoons shining, and raised the largest potatoes and the brightest hollyhocks in Baltimore.

But all Baltimore was not as peaceful as the Pickersgill flag shop. What seemed at first to be the thunder of a summer storm was the roar of British and American ships' guns. After two years of sea warfare, American ships had begun to imitate the methods of pirates. Many of the vessels sailing up and down the Atlantic Coast were now privateers, a polite name for prize-runners. "If British ships can impress our sailors, we will take their cargoes," these privateers said.

A quarrel between nations, which might have been settled peacefully two years before, had blazed into warfare, and at last Baltimore was threatened. British ships seeking a fleet of American privateers were on their way to attack and hold the tiny brick fort which stood on a low peninsula guarding the town. There seemed no hope for Baltimore. Danger such as the towns-people had not known since the Revolution stalked at their very doorsteps.

But it was adventure, not danger, that lifted the brass knocker of Caroline Pickersgill's front door on that long-ago August day. She ran to open it, and curtsied as three townsmen entered in haste and excitement. They were the three officers in charge of the few troops that Baltimore had been able to muster. Their swords hung at their sides, their anxious faces were gray in the candlelight, as they spoke to Caroline's mother.

"Fort McHenry will not stand a day's siege from British guns," they said. "Our only chance is to trick the enemy into thinking us stronger than we are. We desire, Mistress Pickersgill, that you make at once a great American flag. We want this banner to measure at least thirty-six feet long and twenty-nine feet wide. Four hundred yards of bunting will be delivered to you here in a few hours if you consent to help us. What say you? Can you deliver this flag to the fort before we are attacked from the sea? We hope that so large a flag will speak to the enemy of the high courage of our land."

"At once, good sirs," Mary Pickersgill answered. "As soon as the bunting arrives, I will begin cutting."

"Do your best, Mary," urged Rebecca, tapping the brick

hearth with her cane. Then going back to her dream world, she said, "Do you not see General Washington and his aides there in our doorway, come to us for a battle flag?"

"Couldn't I help with the sewing?" begged Caroline, her eyes shining with excitement. "Surely, Mother, you can trust me to stitch stripes together."

So the three, old Rebecca, young Mary, younger Caroline, daughters of the Stars and Stripes, promised to do their part in protecting their town.

The mammoth rolls of bunting were delivered at their house promptly that night. But, alas, it was soon discovered that there was not a room large enough for cutting out the Flag. The parts had to be cut to fit exactly, mostly upon the floor. Much of the sewing also was done on the floor, Mary Pickersgill kneeling down and stitching each stripe, each star. What should they do? At last, in the early morning, with the help of soldiers, they carried the bunting to a deserted malt house that stood near the fort. There, on the great floor, Mary cut, basted, and stitched. Caroline ran between the malt house and their home, taking stripes to be stitched, caring for old Rebecca, and returning to kneel beside her mother and help with the Flag.

The Flag had not been started a moment too soon. Disturbances in Baltimore had begun. A group of British soldiers had broken into the garden of Dr. Beans, a well-known townsman, while he was serving tea to some friends. The doctor had been arrested, and imprisoned on one of the enemy ships as a British prisoner of war. Ladies in crinoline and silks had scattered, leaving their jasmine tea, sponge cakes, and ices untouched. A gentleman guest, young Francis Scott Key, a Baltimore attorney, had gone at once with a flag of truce to attempt the doctor's rescue. He was now aboard the American ship, the *Minden,* in Chesapeake Bay two miles from the town. Should the attack upon

STAR-SPANGLED

Baltimore from the water be successful, it was rumored that the town would be set on fire.

But the Flag was finished— red, white, and blue, six times as long as a man is tall, secure against storms because of the firm hand-stitching of Caroline and her mother, and bright with courage. They watched it being carried to Fort McHenry and raised upon a tall pole behind the guns.

In the early morning after the flag-raising, the attack upon Baltimore from the water began. For twenty-four hours enemy ships poured bombs, rockets, and red-hot shot against the fort, tearing gaping holes in the earth, and piercing the brick walls. A few rents were made in the Flag but it waved bravely in the sunshine. Never had such a flag taken part in battle. Aloof and peaceful, it floated above the fire of the attack. After a day and a night of terrible shellfire, the fort still stood. The great banner stitched by Mary and Caroline Pickersgill billowed in the wind as the attacking fleet sailed away.

From the water, Francis Scott

BANNER GIRL

Key watched the Flag all that night, as it flew above the red of the rockets and the smoke of the bombs. He could not tell whether the British or the American forces were victorious. In the morning of its triumph, when he and Dr. Beans were safe on land again, he wrote a poem about the Flag.

Oh, say can you see by the dawn's early
    light,
What so proudly we hailed at the twi-
    light's last gleaming?

There were many stanzas to the poem, but each ended:

The Star-Spangled Banner, oh, long may
    it wave,
O'er the land of the free and the home
    of the brave.

Soon, everybody in our country was singing Mr. Key's song about the Flag that Caroline had helped to stitch. We still sing "The Star-Spangled Banner," and the old Flag itself is kept as one of our most precious relics of American history in the Smithsonian Institution at Washington. The boy or girl who visits there will marvel at the tiny stitches Caroline set in the star-spangled banner.

From *Children of the Handicrafts*

39

Jack-o'-Lantern

By Ruth H. Colby

"MOTHER, can't I even light a candle in it?" Jonathan Wheeler spoke pleadingly.

"You know your father doesn't like such things."

"I know, Mother. They were wrong when he was little. But even Parson Smith said we might frolic this Halloween. Father—" he hesitated and then brought it out firmly, "Father's old-fashioned."

"You mustn't speak disrespectfully, Jonathan," his mother said.

"But it's such a beauty, Mother!" said Jonathan's sister, Prudence. "It has a mouth full of teeth and great big eyes."

"Prudence," her mother's voice was gentle, "Father doesn't hold with these newfangled ideas. He thinks that Halloween is a heathen festival, as indeed it was once. He doesn't want any jack-o'-lanterns in this house."

"So I can't even light a candle in it." Jonathan's mouth turned down at the corners.

He himself had picked the huge yellow pumpkin from the south meadow, had scooped it out, and carefully cut the big eyes and nose and grinning, tooth-filled mouth. Leslie Faxton, the boy who had just come from England, had shown him how. He had hardly been able to wait for Halloween to light up the huge face. And now he would never know how that mouth would look with a flame back of it.

In the little Puritan town of Quambog, Halloween had never been celebrated. Many of the older people still opposed its holiday merriment. Some even thought that the new parson was much too young and much too newfangled in his ways.

Mrs. Wheeler saw the down-turned mouth.

"They say a ship is in Stonington," she said, "and that in the cargo are oranges. Perhaps I can get you one apiece."

"What are oranges, Mother?"

"Fruit, dear, yellow, and most healthful, they say."

"Like pumpkins, Mother?"

"No, dear, not at all. Wait till you see one. I shall be back before dark. But, Prudence, you might set the table and heat the cornmeal mush. Perhaps you might scrape a little maple sugar. The blue sugar bowl is almost empty."

Two faces still looked downcast.

shapes stealing through the shadows.

"Prue, it's Injun Jim! Probably his brother Joe is with him!"

"Oh, let's get in quick!" Prue fairly flew up in the meadow, Jon right behind her.

There were few Indians left in Quambog, and those few were quiet peaceable folk. Indian Jim was the one bad character. He was apt to steal whatever he could lay his hands on. He and his brother Joe were sometimes ugly in their speech.

"Quick, bar the door, Jon!"

Jon needed no urging. The heavy bar, rarely used, was pushed into place, and Prudence felt a little comforted. It looked so strong. The old house had stood off Indian attacks before.

"The shutters, Jon!"

The two children closed the heavy wooden shutters. The room was quite dark now except for firelight.

From force of habit Prue set the cornmeal mush on the hearth to warm. She wondered who would eat it. If only Father and Mother would come! But there were no welcome sounds of hooves or wheels. Instead the silence seemed to grow heavier. It was getting almost too dark to see each other.

"It's a funny Halloween, Prue." Jon managed a grin.

"Remember how Leslie Faxton told us about witches and how they scared—"

Jon seized Prue. "I've got it, Prue! Get a candle! Quick!"

He raced down cellar. Prudence felt her heart beat faster when she was left alone in the room. But she found a candle.

Jon puffed up the cellar stairs. In his arms, tightly clasped, was the big jack-o'-lantern.

"Quick, Prue, the north room where there's no firelight. We can see the Indians leave Darkhollow if we watch. Shield your candle."

They tiptoed into the north room. It was very dark. Jon set the

44

big jack-o'-lantern on the floor. Then he took the candle and fastened it inside the pumpkin. The great grinning face fairly leaped out at them in the darkness. Both children gazed at it, fascinated, and just a little horrified, for this was the first jack-o'-lantern they had ever seen. It was a fiery goblin, as Leslie Faxton had said. And Father didn't believe in it.

Jon knelt by the window. "Watch closely. We can see anyone against the sky. Most likely, Jim and his brother will go to the barn first, to see what they can take."

"Oh, would they take my Daisy calf?" said Prue.

"She's a good calf." Jon sounded so much like Father that ordinarily Prue would have smiled. Now she was too worried.

Jon clutched her arm. "Isn't that something moving, Prue? There, just leaving the bushes!"

They could just make out two figures close together. The Indians were stealing toward the big barn. That brought them face to face with the front of the house.

Jon, his jaw set firmly, lifted the lighted jack-o'-lantern and set it on the windowsill, its fiery face outward . . . .

Judge and Mrs. Wheeler were glad to be so near home.

"The house is all dark, Father," said Mrs. Wheeler. "How queer!"

Before her husband could answer, a grinning, glowing face appeared out of the darkness. Mrs. Wheeler gasped. It *did* look like a fiery monster suspended in the air, grinning.

Judge Wheeler shut his lips tightly. Jonathan should . . .

Two blood-curdling, high-pitched yells cut through the still night air. There was a sound of swift, running feet. Two dark shapes bounded by the carriage, as the frightened horses dashed up the lane. The Judge had all he could do to hold them.

Mrs. Wheeler, white-faced, flung herself at the door. She heard a heavy bar pushed back. There on the threshold was Prue, sobbing, and Jon, his jaw still shut tight, trembling a little. They flung themselves into her arms.

It was the merriest supper the Wheelers ever had.

Prudence's sumach dress glowed like the deep blooms in the fall. Along the edge of the mantel were brown oak leaves and the trailing fairy wool of clematis vines. On the mantel were red apples, polished like red glass. Between them was a strange new fruit, orange balls about the same size. Jon and Prue thought them beautiful.

But in the center of the table, in the place of honor, on Grandmother's pewter platter, was a fiery-faced jack-o'-lantern with a great wide smile.

Judge Wheeler's smile was almost as wide.

Indians for Thanksgiving

By Dorothy Heiderstadt

IT WAS Thanksgiving Day in New England in 1631. Betsy and her sister, Prudence, lived in a log cabin on the edge of the forest, and they had been left at home while their mother and father went to church. They had wanted to go along, but their father had said the snow was too deep, and Betsy had a cold.

"Be good," he said, as he shouldered his gun. "Keep the fire going and the turkey basting, and keep the doors shut."

The doors had to be kept shut and bolted for the same reason their father had to carry a gun. Indians lurked in the forest—Indians with painted faces, bows and arrows, and tomahawks.

Betsy and Prudence had never seen any of the Indians. Red Squirrel and the people of his tribe had been friendly to the white people. But they had moved away almost a year before.

The two sisters peered through the window and watched their parents going down the path toward the church three miles away. If you have ever seen pictures of the Pilgrims going to church, you will know exactly how they looked—the father dressed in his black suit with the wide white collar and the wide white cuffs, with his tall hat on his head, his silver-buckled shoes on his feet, and his long gun on his shoulder; their mother in her gray cloak lined with blue, with the skirt of her very long gray dress showing beneath, her little gray cap on her head, and her Bible in her hand.

"I wish I could have gone along," sighed Betsy. "Maybe I would have seen an Indian."

"Betsy!" Prudence frowned sternly at her younger sister. "You wouldn't want to see an Indian. The only kind of Indian you would be likely to see in this forest would probably try to scalp you with his tomahawk."

"Red Squirrel wasn't that kind," protested Betsy.

"There aren't many Indians like Red Squirrel," said Prudence. "Come. I'm going to baste the turkey, and you'll have to help."

The turkey was roasting on a pole set across the fireplace. While Betsy held the long-handled saucepan beneath the turkey, Prudence poured spoonfuls of water from the pan onto the turkey. This kept the meat from becoming too dry as it roasted.

By and by, when the turkey had been basted enough, Betsy put down the saucepan and went back to the window. The forest lay cold and still in the gray light of the winter morning. It was beginning to snow again. "Just the same, I would like to see an Indian. Not a big one," she went on hastily. "Just a little one would do. One of Red Squirrel's children."

Betsy had missed Red Squirrel's children, since they moved away. She had no other playmates now except her sister. And Prudence, though she was only ten, seemed quite grown up. She refused to play with dolls any more, and much preferred to bake and knit.

Just now she was knitting a muffler for her father, and her needles clicked industriously as she sat before the fire. Betsy felt uneasy. She was getting to be a big girl, and she knew that she would soon have to learn to knit. She was sure that she could never learn to do it as it ought to be done.

Betsy sighed and began looking out the window again. The morning seemed very long. The good smell of roast turkey filled the room, and her mouth watered. Two hours until dinnertime! How could she wait? If she could only have some of it now! If she could only see an Indian!

Suddenly she gasped. Something was moving out there among the trees, something quite small and close to the ground. It looked like a little boy.

"Prudence!" she cried excitedly. "Look! Look! An Indian!"

Prudence dropped her knitting. "Where?" she gasped. Visions of tomahawks and war paint ran through her head.

"There! See?" whispered Betsy, pointing. Just at that moment a little Indian boy came out of the forest all alone. He was about five years old, and he had a round, fat face and two bright black eyes. He was wrapped in a bright blanket, and he was floundering through the snow toward the house.

"It must be one of Red Squirrel's children!" cried Prudence. "That means Red Squirrel has come back."

"Of course, that isn't any of Red Squirrel's children," said Betsy scornfully. "Don't I know exactly what every one of them looks like? This is a strange Indian. Oh, look at him. Prudence! Isn't he cunning?"

The little Indian was standing within a few feet of the door.

He looked around and stamped the snow off his moccasined feet.

"Let's get him to come in!" said Betsy. "Maybe he's lost. Maybe he's hungry."

Prudence went to the door and opened it. "Do come in!" she said politely. "I'm sure you must be cold out there."

"Oh, Prudence!" Betsy laughed, and ran over to stand beside her. "He doesn't understand what we say."

They beckoned, but the little Indian only looked at them solemnly. Perhaps he had never seen two girls in long gray dresses, white aprons, and buckled shoes. Perhaps he had never seen a house before. He stood there staring.

Then, just as they were beginning to wonder what to do next, he walked past them into the house. There, he continued to look curiously around him—at the ceiling of the room, at the chairs, the table, the spinning wheel, and the fireplace.

At sight of the fireplace, his eyes sparkled. He went close and held out his hands to the blaze. He sniffed the air hungrily, and Betsy, watching him, felt a pang of hunger too.

"I believe he's hungry," said Prudence. "We must give him something to eat."

INDIANS FOR THANKSGIVING

"Perhaps we ought to eat with him," suggested Betsy quickly, "so he won't feel impolite to be eating there in front of us."

"And leave Father and Mother to eat their Thanksgiving dinner alone?" demanded Prudence in a shocked voice.

"That's right. We couldn't do it," said Betsy.

The table was already set for dinner, although it would be quite a while before their father and mother would be home. Prudence and Betsy carved a piece off the turkey, and put it on a plate. They put a big spoonful of sauce beside it and one of potatoes and gravy. Then they helped the little Indian off with his blanket, and put him in front of the table in a chair.

All this time, he had not said one word. He allowed them to lift him into his chair. But he looked uncertainly at the food on his plate. He picked up the turkey in his hands, and took a bite. Then he laid it down and reached out a hand to pick up the potatoes and gravy the same way.

"Wait!" cried Prudence, and he drew back his hand quickly. "He doesn't know how to eat. We'll have to feed him."

So they took turns feeding their small guest. First, Prudence would put a spoonful of potatoes and gravy into his mouth. When he had swallowed that, Betsy would put in a spoonful of sauce. Then the little Indian would take a bite of turkey, and then a bite of bread. They made a game out of it, and presently he was laughing so much that he could scarcely eat.

Suddenly, in the midst of the game, he looked at the window and gave a pleased, excited cry. He pointed and began to talk very fast in his own language. He struggled to get down out of his chair.

Betsy and Prudence, somewhat surprised, helped him down and followed him to the window. He peered out of it, talking eagerly. He kept looking up at them to see whether they understood. He even grew a little impatient because they could not

understand.

Outside, the snow was falling fast, but the girls saw nothing unusual out of the window. Prudence wondered uneasily what the little Indian had seen. Suppose big Indians had looked in—the kind who were wild and carried tomahawks and scalped people! Suppose this was the child of that sort of Indian! She began to wish that her parents would hurry home.

The little Indian, however, shrugged his shoulders at last and returned to his interrupted meal. When he had eaten everything on his plate, his head began to nod and he leaned against Prudence's shoulder.

"He's gone to sleep," she whispered.

With much careful tugging and pulling, the girls managed to carry their guest over to the old settle. There he slept peacefully. After clearing away his place at the table, they sat down before the fire. Prudence threw on some more sticks and took up her knitting. Betsy, on a low footstool close to the old settle, looked at the little Indian.

"Isn't he nice?" she whispered. "His tribe must be camping in the forest. I suppose he wandered off and got lost. I imagine his mother is worried, don't you? He's so little."

"I only hope," said Prudence, "that when they find him here they won't think we were trying to steal him, and tear the house down over our heads."

"They won't do that," said Betsy softly. "He will tell them

INDIANS FOR THANKSGIVING

that we are his friends, and that we gave him part of our Thanksgiving dinner. I hope he's going to live here in the forest. Then we can play with him, and we won't miss Red Squirrel's children so. I've missed them dreadfully."

"And a good thing they went away," Prudence. "A great girl like you, who should have learned to knit and bake long ago, playing around with Indians!"

But she smiled at her sister as she said this. Betsy, who knew that Prudence was not so stern as she sounded, smiled back at her.

"Dear me!" said Prudence suddenly. "I'm a little tired of knitting, myself, right now. I think I'll rest awhile." And she drew her own footstool up close to the settle, and leaned against it as Betsy was doing.

So warm was the room, so drowsy was the sound of the fire purring and crackling on the hearth, that in a few minutes both sisters were also fast asleep. They were not aware that someone had slipped up to the cabin.

When Betsy's father and mother came down the forest path on their way home from church, they saw several Indians looking in at their front window. The father, badly frightened, shifted his gun under his arm and started forward quickly.

"Wait!" said his wife in a low voice. "Let us see if they are friendly. Speak to them first!"

At the sound of her voice, one of the Indians turned. The father, much to his relief, recognized Red Squirrel. The other Indians also turned, and Red Squirrel spoke to them. Then he came forward to greet his friends, the two white people. Silently he made signs for them to look in at the window.

Wondering, they did so. Inside the big room they saw the fire burning on the hearth, the kettle steaming cheerfully, and the table set for Thanksgiving. They saw their daughters fast asleep beside the settle. They saw the little Indian stretched out comfortably on top of the settle.

One of the strange Indians, who was wearing a large and imposing feather war bonnet, began to talk very fast. He talked for quite a long time, and then stopped suddenly. He looked at Betsy's and Prudence's father and mother, with snapping black eyes. He seemed to be waiting.

"He says," began Red Squirrel, "that he is White Bear, who rules a powerful tribe of the Pequot Indians. This morning, the braves in his tribe were to go on the warpath against the white people who live in this forest. As they were leaving, it was discovered that the son of the chief was gone. He had wandered away. Then this big snow began to fall, and they were afraid that they might not find him again.

"One of them heard the sound of children laughing in this cabin, and looked in at this window. There he saw the chief's son eating at your table. He ran and told the chief.

"Do you understand what your children have done? They have taken in a child of their enemies and warmed him at their fire. He was hungry, and they fed him. White Bear says he will not forget this. From this day, he will be the friend of the white people of this forest, just as I am their friend.

INDIANS FOR THANKSGIVING

"When I heard that he was coming to make war on the white people, I came as quickly as I could to see if I could not persuade him to stop. Now it is not necessary. Your children have persuaded him, because they have been kind to his son."

When Red Squirrel had finished speaking, the white man held out his hand.

"Come in," he said, "and share our Thanksgiving dinner."

The Indians entered the cabin with great dignity. Betsy, who was the first to awake, was at first terrified and then delighted when she saw all the Indians. Even Prudence was thrilled over sitting down to dinner with a real Indian chief.

The Indian boy, whose name was Little Wolf, was delighted to see his father. Although he had already been given one Thanksgiving dinner, he found that he was able to eat another.

After that, Betsy had a wonderful time. She had twice as many Indian children to play with as before. She had the children of Red Squirrel's tribe and

the children of White Bear's tribe. The powerful tribe of White Bear lived near by in the forest for many years. And every Thanksgiving Day, White Bear and Little Wolf and Red Squirrel and several other Indians came to Betsy's and Prudence's house for dinner.

Christmas Eve on Beacon Hill

A Story of Boston

By Frances Cavanah

BENJY was very lonely after he went to live with his aunt in a stately house on Beacon Hill. He missed his father, who was away at war, and he missed his friends back in Chicago. He knew that Aunt Prue had tried to keep him from being homesick. She had taken him on sightseeing trips and had told him so much about the city that he was afraid he would burst with information. But what he wanted most was a boy his own age to play with.

Then, one day down in the Common, he met Tony. Tony's father had been born in Italy and he lived in the North End, near the house where Paul Revere once lived. Tony loved Boston and earned many dimes and quarters showing sightseers around.

Soon he and Benjy were "in business" together.

Benjy worked hard at his lessons all week, but on Saturday after lunch he hurried to the North End. Being a guide was fun, and business was brisk. Sometimes he earned seventy-five cents in an afternoon, and it was almost more than he could bear not to talk of his success at home. Several times he started to tell Aunt Prue about Tony, but he did not quite dare.

By Thanksgiving, when the first snow blanketed the city, Benjy had earned nearly four dollars, and he had saved every cent of his November allowance. Christmas boxes for men overseas had to be mailed before the first of December, and he felt rich when he went shopping with seven dollars in his pocket, After buying Dad a compass he had enough money left for a box of raisins, several chocolate bars, and such gifts as razor blades and soap, which the men overseas needed. He wrapped each present in blue paper sprinkled with silver stars and tied it with silver ribbon. Johanna, the Irish housekeeper, added a fruitcake. After the packages had been placed in a shoe box, she filled the corners with lumps of sugar.

"Faith, 'tis a lonesome feeling not to know where your fayther is this Christmastime," she said, brushing the back of her hand across her eyes.

Benjy held his chin very firm as he wrapped the shoe box in heavy brown paper. He addressed it to Lieutenant John Lawrence, in care of the Postmaster in New York City. "I'm glad the Postmaster knows," he said.

"That is the spirit," said Aunt Prue. "I am pleased, Benjamin John, to see how wisely you used your November allowance. I don't see how you managed to buy so many gifts. Are you looking forward to your first Christmas Eve on Beacon Hill?"

"Well, you see, Aunt Prue—" Benjy blushed. "There's something I want to tell you—I mean ask you. Are you going to have Open House this year?"

"To be sure. I always have Open House on Christmas Eve."

"Do—do many people come?"

"About twenty-five. The same friends and relatives who have been coming to my Open House for years."

"Don't you ever have anybody *new*?" asked Benjy in dismay.

Aunt Prue smiled a little. "Only you, Benjamin John. And you're not really new, because you are my own grandnephew."

"Oh!" said Benjy flatly. He had invited Tony to Open House one day, and the next minute had regretted the invitation. He was not quite sure that his aunt would approve, and for a while he had hoped that Tony would forget. But Tony had not forgotten. Just last Saturday he had been saying how nice the houses on the Hill looked on Christmas Eve.

The first of the month Aunt Prue gave Benjy his December allowance. He used part of the money to buy her a dainty little china cat and four china kittens for her collection of figures on the parlor whatnot. If he could only give them to her now, it might be easier to ask about Tony. But he couldn't give a Christmas present before Christmas, and Open House was held on Christmas Eve.

As the weather grew colder, few sightseers ventured out into the raw east wind that blew in from the ocean. No one wanted to hire two boys as guides, and they began going down to the Common to play. The elm trees, their branches sheathed in ice, glittered in the winter sunshine. The shouts of the children skating on the Frog Pond sounded high and shrill in the thin, cold air.

"I had a letter from Pop," said Tony the Saturday before Christmas, as the boys sat down on a bench near the pond to put on their skates. "I guess a fellow couldn't have a nicer Christmas gift than that."

"That's right," said Benjy and suddenly felt very lonely. It had been such a long time since he had heard from Dad.

"I had told Pop that—that you—"Tony hesitated—"that you had invited me to Open House. He thought it was just swell. You still want me to come, don't you?"

"Why, of course," said Benjy, more confidently than he was feeling. To himself he added, "I just *have* to tell Aunt Prue tonight."

But when he reached home there were guests for dinner. The next day Aunt Prue was busy making plans for Open House, and Benjy put off telling her. The day after that it was the same, until finally it was the afternoon of Christmas Eve.

"Benjamin John," said Aunt Prue. "Will you please help me

with these candles?"

Under her careful direction, Benjy placed tall white candles in rows of silver candlesticks on the sills and on the upper sash of every window. Then she sent him down to the florist to buy another wreath of holly. When he came back Johanna had covered the long mahogany table in the dining room with the embroidered cloth that Aunt Prue's seafaring grandfather had brought from China. Aunt Prue was arranging a big bowl of holly as a centerpiece, flanked on either side by red candles in tall, branched candlesticks.

"I am going to my room to lie down," she said, drawing her Paisley shawl a little closer. "I must be refreshed to meet my guests tonight."

"What if—if somebody extra came in?" asked Benjy. "Would there be—enough to eat?"

"Please, Benjamin John!" Aunt Prue was already halfway up the stairs. "Don't bother me with foolish questions. There will be no extra guests tonight."

Benjy's heart seemed to drop

61

down into his shoes.

After dinner, Johanna kindled a taper and Benjy went from window to window lighting the candles. From the third floor to the first he made his rounds, until every window was ablaze with light. In the houses across the street—in nearly every house upon the Hill—soft candlelight shone out upon the snow. The curtains had been parted in many of the windows, so that hundreds of visitors who thronged the sidewalks on Christmas Eve might see the handsome rooms with their fine old furniture and lovely paintings. In this way the people of Beacon Hill shared their houses with the passers-by.

Shortly after seven the strains of "Holy Night" were borne across the frosty air as the first group of carolers started up the Hill. By half past seven Aunt Prue's parlors were filled with guests. Benjy met aunts and uncles, and great-aunts and aunts by marriage, and cousins, and cousins once removed, until he was dizzy trying to remember their names.

As he padded among the guests with plates of sandwiches and platters heaped high with star-shaped cookies, he kept listening for the knocker on the front door. Time and again it fell with a dull thud and Johanna ushered another guest into the parlor. Perhaps Tony wasn't coming after all.

"Hi-ya, Benjy! Here I am."

Everyone turned to look at Tony, brushed and scrubbed within an inch of his life, stand-

62

ing in the doorway. Benjy set a plate of sandwiches down on a marble-topped table and hurried across the room.

"Hello, Tony." His voice quavered, but he took Tony by the elbow and led him over to the divan where Aunt Prue was sitting with a bald-headed gentleman named "Cousin Jonathan."

"Aunt Prue," said Benjy, "this is my friend, Tony Vallento."

Tony held his head high, but Aunt Prue looked into his dark eyes and knew that he was frightened. She hesitated. Then: "Welcome, Tony Vallento," she said, holding out her hand. "Johanner, please bring a cup of hot chocolate for our guest."

"Good evening, Miss Lawrence. It was swell—nice—" Tony was choosing his words carefully— "of you to invite me here."

"Have you and Tony known each other long?" she asked.

"We were in business together until it got so cold." Tony seemed surprised that she did not know. "I live near Paul Revere's house and I show sightseers around. I introduced Benjy as the boy whose uncle knew Paul Revere and he recited the poem."

"Benjamin John," said Cousin Jonathan, "if your face gets any redder, it's going to catch on fire."

To Benjy's relief, Johanna returned with a cup of chocolate on a silver tray, and Cousin Jonathan gave Tony his place on the divan. For the next ten minutes Tony was very busy with sandwiches and star-shaped cookies, but not too busy to talk.

"Can you beat it—Benjy didn't used to like Boston. He didn't like history, but now he can reel it off like nobody's

CHRISTMAS EVE

carolers, Benjy—though he had known that Beacon Hill was beautiful—had never known that it could be so beautiful as this. There was a wreath on nearly every door, and the streets were two blazing lines of light.

In Louisburg Square the carolers paused at one end of the little park. The leader struck a note on his tuning fork, and they began to sing:

"*O little town of Bethlehem.*" The people on the sidewalks listened in silence, and the statue of Columbus seemed to look down benignly from his pedestal.

"I have to go now," said Tony reluctantly. "I had a nice time, Benjy. Your aunt is just swell."

When Benjy reached home, the last guest had gone. Aunt Prue picked up a letter from the marble-topped table. "This just came air mail, special delivery," she said.

Benjy tore the letter open. He pored over the pages, as though he could not read them fast enough. "Oh, boy, it's from Dad. He's in London, Aunt Prue.

ON BEACON HILL

Listen, what he says:

> I've been invited to have Christmas dinner with friends who live in an old London square that is a dead ringer for Louisburg Square.

Benjy turned a page, and there was a catch in his voice as he went on reading:

> I hope you like Boston better than you did, Benjy. Some wise man once said that Boston was more than a city, that it was a way of feeling. I think Boston is a way of feeling about our country. Probably this is because it has done so much to make the history of our country.

Benjy laid the letter down. "I *do* like Boston now, I sort of feel that it belongs to me—just the way Tony does."

Aunt Prue looked at her nephew with an odd smile. "Tony seems to have done what I failed to do. He's made you a good Bostonian. He—he's a fine boy."

"Oh, he likes you, too, Aunt Prue," said Benjy earnestly. "He thinks you're swell—and I do, too."

Aunt Prue grew pink and then crimson. But all she said was, "Thank you, Benjy. A gentleman hasn't paid me a compliment like that in years."

He looked at her in astonishment. She had never called him anything but Benjamin John before.

Together they walked over to the window. A group of carolers had gathered on the sidewalk. The candlelight fell softly on their upturned faces as they sang:

> Silent night, holy night,
> All is calm, all is bright.

Benjy felt his father's letter in his pocket. Then he slipped his free hand into Aunt Prue's.

Adapted from Benjy of Boston

Christmas in the Piney Woods

A STORY OF THE ARKANSAS HILLS

By CHARLIE MAY SIMON

ALL DAY on Christmas Eve it had been raining, making a pattering sound on the roof, beating against the window, and trickling through the rag of a quilt stuffed in the broken pane. The ruts became puddles big enough for the ducks to splash around in. It was raining inside, too, fast filling up the tub on the floor with little drops that came from a leak in the roof. One of the beds had to be moved closer to the middle of the room.

Melissa stood on tiptoe, pressing her nose against the pane, looking out at the tall pines rocking this way and that. The chickens were huddled together in the shed and the calf leaned over the fence of the lot and bawled for his mamma.

"Will Santa Claus come tonight in all this rain?" Melissa asked, turning to her mamma, who sat by the fire, churning.

Mamma smiled gently.

"I'm afraid not, honey," she said. "I'm afraid he'd have a right hard time making the crossing."

"Is that child at it again?" Papa said, coming through the doorway with his arms loaded with wood. "I declare she's getting plumb worrisome here lately."

CHRISTMAS IN THE PINEY WOODS

Christmas had meant little to Melissa until this year when Lige, her father, decided to take his cotton to the big city where it would bring a better price. He took Melissa and her mamma, Marthy, with him. What fun they had, sitting in the wagon yard eating their lunch from the tin lard bucket, and watching the many people and automobiles pass! Later they walked up and down Main Street, looking in the gay windows.

There was a Christmas tree in one of the windows, bright and shining, and Melissa had wanted to stand long and look. They went inside the store, and while Papa and Mamma were buying flour and sugar and baking soda, Melissa saw a doll in a box. It had short, yellow hair and eyes that opened and shut; and when she picked it up, it gave a little cry. She held it close, and her heart was bursting with joy.

"Look here, little one," the storekeeper said coming toward her, "those toys are not to be handled."

He took the doll from her and put it in the box, but when he turned around and looked at her, he smiled.

"Never mind," he said. "Maybe Santa Claus will have one for you this Christmas." And he gave her a card with a picture of Santa Claus on it, in a red suit and a white beard and a jolly laugh, looking for all the world like old Daddy Hawkins who played the fiddle and sang songs at parties.

And ever after that, to this day, Melissa had been worrying her mamma, asking how many days more until Christmas.

After the supper things were done, and the fire was

low, Mamma put some sweet potatoes in the ashes, and some black-eyed peas in the iron pot over the fire. On a string from the mantel she hung a chicken that Papa had killed and plucked. The heat of the fire turned the chicken around and around, so that by morning it would be roasted a golden brown.

"And because tomorrow's Christmas," Mamma said, "we'll have a blackberry cobbler pie and I'll open a jar of watermelon rind preserves."

Then they all washed their feet in the tin wash pan by the fire, and got into bed.

No sooner had she fallen asleep, it seemed, than Melissa was awakened by a gentle shake of her shoulder.

"Wake up, little one," her papa was saying. "Mamma is feeling puny, and I'm bound to hitch up old Beck and fetch the granny woman."

Melissa rubbed the sleep out of her eyes.

"You don't have to get up," Papa said. "Just watch over your mamma and don't bother her. I'll be back directly." He put some pine knots on the ashes and built up a roaring fire.

The fire flickered and cast queer shadows on the newspaper-covered walls. The chicken turned fast and furiously and the peas in the pot boiled loudly. Melissa got up and raked out the sweet potatoes and dragged the iron pot onto the hearth, and she tied a knot in the string to hang the chicken higher.

Mamma looked pale and

THE PINEY WOODS

gaunt with her dark hair hanging loose over her shoulders. Her eyes were closed, but Melissa knew she was not sleeping. She wanted to get in bed with her mamma and put her arms around her and kiss her tired cheeks. But Papa had said she must not be bothered, so Melissa got into her own bed and lay quietly waiting.

Gusts of wind blew through the cracks of the wall. Melissa lay in the darkness, getting up from time to time to add more pine knots to the fire. Finally, after long hours of waiting, a rooster crowed, and the hound dog stirred from his bed under the house, rubbing against the floor boards as he moved. Directly Melissa heard the pattering of hoofs, and before she could slip her dress on over her petticoat, Lige came into the room. Behind him was the granny woman, her hair stringing down under her hat and her skirts dripping with water.

She nodded to Mamma and went over by the fire to dry, shivering and rubbing her rough old hands together. Papa bent down over Mamma and kissed her gently on the forehead.

The granny woman began to step around briskly. She sent Papa out to the woods to fetch some bark from the north side of a red oak, and some black haw roots, to brew a tea.

"And, Melissa," she said, "put on a kettle of water to boil."

Melissa had to draw fresh water from the well, as there was none in the water bucket. It splashed on her bare feet and made her toes ache with cold as she poured it into the kettle.

And when Papa brought back the herbs, he said to Melissa,

"Come, little one, Granny can do for your mamma, and you and I will go out and get us some Christmas fixings."

Melissa wanted to stay, but her papa made her put on her shoes, and he wrapped Mamma's big coat around her. The sleeves flapped down over her hands, and the bottom came down to her feet, so that she had to hold it high to keep from stumbling. The old hound dog started after them, then turned back to the house and stayed where he was.

The mules, tethered to the oak post in the front yard, were still nervous and wet from swimming the swollen creek. Lige led them to the barn and fed them some corn. The speckled hen that slept under the house clucked, and her ten half-grown chickens came running after her and pecked at each grain the mules dropped. All the stars had disappeared except one, which shone down on them brighter than ever.

"Don't you reckon we'd best be going on back now?" Melissa asked, turning back to the little cabin on the hillside. It looked bare and alone, the flowers in lard buckets on the porch shelf were drooping and brown, and the rambler bush clung to the chimney with cold bare branches.

Lige picked some scarlet berries from a haw bush.

"Folks out yonder in the lowlands use

THE PINEY WOODS

this stuff to keep Christmas,"
he said. "They hang it with holly
and mistletoe in their windows,
and it makes the room right
pretty and gay."

He picked branches of the
berries and gave them to Melissa.
Then he carried her high on his
shoulders to the sycamore tree
behind the barn, and Melissa
reached up and picked the mistletoe that was clinging fast to
the truck.

The little black pig, looking
for an early morning breakfast,
followed behind them, making
a long furrow in the soft mud
with his nose.

"And now," Papa said, "take
your mistletoe and haw berries
to the cotton shed. Then go to
the potato house and fetch some
peanuts and popcorn, and get
some pine cones from the ground.
We'll have as fine a Christmas
as e'er a body could have. I'll be
back directly." He strode off to
the house with long steps.

The early morning air was
cold, and Melissa was shivering
and her nose and fingers were
red when Papa came back. He

73

seemed worried, as if he might turn gruff at any minute, until he looked down at Melissa.

"Why, you're freezing, little one," he said. "Why didn't you say something? Here, I'll build us a fire."

When the fire was roaring and warm, and they were seated close to it under the cotton shed, Papa shelled some popcorn and popped it in the iron skillet he brought back with him. Then he took a needle and thread from his jumper pocket and showed Melissa how to string the peanuts and popcorn.

It was such a pretty string, and the fire was so warm and comfortable, that Melissa almost forgot why she had that queer little ache in her heart. She looked out over the long, even rows of cotton plants, now bare and brown, and bent down by the winter wind. It seemed long ago when they were tiny green things, and she had helped weed them with her hoe. Mamma was with them then, laughing and funning, and making believe Melissa could chop twice as many weeds as she or Papa.

Melissa wanted to say to her papa that she had changed her mind about keeping Christmas. She didn't care any more about

74

the doll that could open and shut its eyes and cry. All she wanted now was to be with her mamma, to feel her sturdy arms about her again. She started to get up and run to the house, but Lige held her firmly by the hand.

"Not yet, little one," he said.

He led her to the piney woods where he gathered branches of holly and he cut down a young cedar. And again they sat by the fire under the cotton shed and tied gay branches of holly and mistletoe and red haw berries, one for each of the windows and some for the doors. Papa sang as they worked, old songs he had learned from his grandmother many years ago, when he was a little one. Melissa's lips trembled and she tried hard to keep the tears from her eyes.

Directly, they heard the granny woman yell for them, and

LOU PETERS

Papa took Melissa up in his arms and walked with long steps toward the house. It didn't look so lonesome now. The smoke curled in big clouds from the chimney and the granny woman's voice was heard inside, crooning and chuckling.

Melissa ran straight to the bed, and her heart warmed to see Mamma smile at her. At her side was a baby, tiny and red, and squinting at her.

"Look, honey," Mamma said, pointing to the baby. "Santa Claus did bring you a doll that closes its eyes and cries."

"Is it mine?" Melissa asked.

"All yours," Mamma replied.

Melissa held out her arms.

CHILDREN OF THE AMERICAS

Bluebonnets for Lucinda

A STORY OF TEXAS

By FRANCES CLARKE SAYERS

HERR GERANIUM, where are the bluebonnets?" asked Lucinda the morning after she arrived. "I've looked about the garden, and there's no blue flower there."

"Ach, you sleepy head," said Herr Geranium. "Last night, when we drove by a field of them, you were sound asleep. But the field is near, and this afternoon, maybe, when I come from town, we will drive to see it."

Lucinda, who lived on Oleander Island in the great blue Gulf of Mexico, was visiting her friends, Herr and Frau Geranium, on the mainland. Although bluebonnets grow almost everywhere in Texas, not a single bluebonnet grew on Oleander Island. And Lucinda wanted to see them.

After breakfast Herr Geranium took her by the hand and led her out to see the farm. It was a tidy little farm, the white house, the red barn, and the giant windmill all snuggled upon the side

78

BLUEBONNETS FOR LUCINDA

of a hill. There were three cows, a flock of speckled chickens, and a pen of little black pigs.

On the crest of the hill, the fig trees stood. Looking down the slope on the other side, Lucinda caught sight of a pond. There were five fine, white geese standing about it.

"Geese!" said Lucinda. "Let's hurry down to see the geese!" But Herr Geranium pulled her back as she started downhill.

"No! No! Lucinda," he cried. "You must not go near the geese. They are fine geese but very cross. When I go to feed them, they run at me, and chase me. They stretch out their long necks and hiss. My beasts, they are all my friends. But the geese, ach, they are terrible. You will stay away from them, *mein kind,* Ja?"

Lucinda called to them. "Hello there," she said. Not a goose turned a feather in her direction. "It's too bad about the geese, Herr Geranium," she said. "I always thought I'd like them."

That afternoon, when Herr Geranium had gone to town and
Frau Geranium was sleeping on the horsehair sofa, Lucinda took
her music box, and went out to the fig orchard. Herr and Frau
Geranium had given her the music box on the day she was six
years old. The top had a picture on it: a picture of a little flaxen-
haired girl sitting under a tree, playing on her flute.

Lucinda climbed up the smooth trunk of a large tree. It was
cool there in the shade of the broad leaves. Below her were the
geese, beautiful in the sun. The old gander stood on one yellow
foot, his head under his wing. One fellow shoved his bill through
the sweet black mud of the pond, his tail feathers twitching with
delight. Another lay in the dust on the ground, worn bare of
grass by the brushing of wings.

"You cross old things!" said Lucinda aloud.

Suddenly she saw something moving downhill, toward the
pond. It was Barnacle, her cat. He sniffed the air. Then slowly,
slowly, paw over paw, he crept down the hill. Lucinda watched
him. On he went, without a sound, until he reached the thorny
shelter of a bramble bush. There he crouched, with gleaming
eyes and switching tail, waiting, waiting. . . .

All of a sudden the gander jerked his head from under his
wing. He saw Barnacle and, honking to the others, he took after

him, wings outspread, neck stretched forward, and a terrible hissing coming from his yellow bill. Barnacle turned like a flash and ran uphill. Fast as he ran, the goose ran faster, and he nipped the tip of Barnacle's tail. Barnacle cried out in pain.

Then Lucinda jumped out of the tree, ran down the hill crying, "Shoo! Shoo!" and waving her arms in the air. She tripped and fell sprawling, and the music box, the beautiful silver music box, went rolling over and over, down the hill. Every time the little knob hit the ground, the tinkling notes of music came tumbling out.

When Lucinda picked herself up, Barnacle was clawing his way up the trunk of a fig tree. But what had happened to the geese! They were no longer angry. They stood, stretching their necks, turning their heads, searching for something lost in the air. Then Lucinda remembered the picture of the goose girl on the music box.

"Oh, it's the music that's changed them," she said and, swooping down among them, she picked up the music box, which was a little dented by the fall, and turned the handle. Out came the tunes, as merrily as ever. One by one the ferocious geese lined up

to her a great bouquet of blue flowers.

"Bluebonnets!" he said. "For Lucinda! She tamed the geese."
Then Herr Geranium said, "I'll come, too," and he joined in,
marching behind Barnacle's tail.

"I'll come, too," shouted Frau Geranium, and she took off
her apron to wave like a banner. So they marched, Lucinda, the
five fat geese, Barnacle with his tail waving, Herr Geranium,
swinging bluebonnets, and Frau Geranium, with her apron for
a flag. Back to the pond they went, and there they left the bewildered geese to stand and wonder what had happened.

84

BLUEBONNETS FOR LUCINDA

That evening, after supper, Herr Geranium hitched Schiller to the buggy, and drove Lucinda to the bluebonnet field. There she saw bluebonnets stretching away across the hills—miles and miles of them, like cascades of bluest water. "I know," said Lucinda. "The bluebonnets grow so that you and Frau Geranium will remember how the Gulf looks in the sun."

And that's the story of how Lucinda saw bluebonnets growing in Texas, in the spring of the year. And how she learned why the goose girl on her music box plays a flute to her geese, who stand quietly, white on a green hill.

From *Bluebonnets for Lucinda*

Juan, the Yaqui

As Told by Kees Chissy, a Navaho boy

By Isis L. Harrington

THE strange boy came to our hogan in the forest at the foot of the Black Mountains one night in early winter. He spoke queer words, not like those of my tribe. He made motions for food as he dropped down on the bearskin near the fire.

My mother gave him food. He ate so fast it was soon gone, and then he fell asleep.

Father and I sat by the fire. We talked low in our language. We knew he could not understand Navaho.

"What a strange boy!"

"Yes," answered my father. "No older than you, yet see how like an old man's his face is. See his heavy shoulders and crooked hands. He is Indian, but of some tribe far off."

As my father talked, Nah Tonny crept into the hogan. Nah Tonny, an old Navaho of our clan, had warred and hunted over all the country to the south. When a young man, he had once been captured by savage Apaches. For five winters he lived in Mexico before he was able to return to our tribe.

"Who?" asked the white-haired man, pointing with his hand in the direction of the boy, as he seated himself.

"A strange boy who wandered to our door tonight," my father answered. "He speaks strange words that have no meaning."

Nah Tonny leaned over and shook the stranger. Then he took from his belt the black tail of a deer and brushed the boy's face. The boy awoke and sat up. Seeing the old man and my father laughing, he laughed, too, and again began his queer words.

"*Amigo, mi Yaqui amigo!*" said Nah Tonny, holding out his hand. The boy threw his arms around the old man's knees.

Then Nah Tonny talked in the strange words learned when he was a captive among the wild Apaches. The boy cried, and held the old man's knees tighter. In a little while the two began to talk together. My father and I waited.

"He is a Yaqui Indian," old Nah Tonny told us, when they had finished talking the queer words. "He speaks his own tongue with Apache words and Spanish words. I used to do that.

"He says," the old man went on, "that he runs away from the gold mines far south, where he digs much yellow sand since a small boy. Always he work. So his father. So his mother. Till they die. He crawl into the desert one night. All day he hide. All night travel. He no more dig for yellow sand."

"*No! No! Mucho trabajo en las minas!*" the boy said, and began to cry again. " 'No! No!' he says," Nah Tonny told us, "'Much work in the mines.' "

"*Su nombre, amigo?*" asked the old man.

"*Jaun, de los Yaquis,*" the boy answered.

"His name is Juan, of the Yaquis," Nah Tonny explained to us. "Let us rest now."

We all lay down. I tried to sleep, but could only think of the stranger near me. The night passed, and when I woke, the boy was up. He had brought wood for the fire and water from the water hole. We were soon seated around the food and Juan of the Yaquis was talking. Only Nah Tonny could understand, but on this morning began the many happy times I was to have with this strange boy. He learned to talk to me in my own Navaho tongue. He learned all the English I could teach him.

When the month of snows had gone and the grass was lifting up the dead leaves, my father called us one morning and said, "The sheep are restless for the mountains. The burro is loaded. Drive the flock high up near the snow. There plenty water. There green grass. You are brave enough?"

I did not answer.

"We are brave enough," came from Juan of the Yaquis. "Your sheep are safe when Juan is there."

"Be careful of the mountain storm that kills the young ones,"

JUAN, THE YAQUI

said my father.

We started on our way, driving the sheep and goats. Our burro walked with the sheep. It took many days to drive the flock high into the Black Mountains. We made camp among the trees whose leaves are never quiet. Here our sheep found grass. The goats climbed high among the rocks to eat the leaves.

Juan of the Yaquis was a good shepherd. He would carry the tired lambs after the mother sheep. He would never kill even a goat for our food. He cried when I killed a lamb that had broken its leg. He wouldn't eat any of the meat. I laughed and called him *Ah ta di zhine* ("He who is not brave").

We had been in the moun-

tains half of the moon when a terrible storm came on. The wind
came like howling wolves. It stung. Our breath piled up in snow
on our breasts. We were far above our camp. I had nothing to
keep me warm. Juan had but a sheepskin he wore tied about his
waist. For a while we hid behind rocks. The sharp snow drove
us out. I wanted to sleep. The Yaqui beat me as he tied his sheepskin about me.

"Go to the camp," he yelled in my ear. "Go straight down.
Keep going. If you do not get to camp, I follow and kill. I kill
now, if you sleep."

Juan looked wild. His heavy hands beat me more.

"Will you keep going and not stop?" he asked. "If you not
reach camp, I follow! I kill! When I come camp and find you, I
not kill! Go, now!"

JUAN, THE YAQUI

I ran. The wind stung my face. The snow cut my eyes. I looked back. Juan watched. He threw a heavy stone. I ran faster.

The sheepskin beat about my head. The wind was louder. The snow was sharper. It blew into piles that covered rocks. It was night—dark. I kept on. Sometimes I fell and was half covered with snow before I could rise. I dared not stop. The Yaqui would kill me if I was not in camp when he came. Maybe he was there now. My father's sheep? The lambs? But I stumbled on in the night. I reached the camp and fell into our shelter. I hid among the sheepskins. I listened for the Yaqui. The wind screamed like eagles. I slept.

When I woke it was no longer dark. I looked around for Juan. He was not there. I crept to the door. The world was strange. Sharp-edged piles of snow lay all about. The thin, strong wind cut them. The snow filled the sky. There was no sun. I ate some dried meat and slept again.

Two terrible nights passed. Our camp was buried but for a small hole. Then the wind became quiet. I crept out. The sun shone. Juan had not come. He would be dead. My father's sheep might be dead, too, but I must find them.

All day I climbed. All was strange and white. There was no trail. The sun was touching a high white mountain to the west when I saw the sheep. They looked black on the snow. I kept on and soon reached them. They were not dead. They were bunched on a place where the snow was tramped hard. There was a wall of snow around them. They ate the green needles from spruce branches pulled from the trees and thrown among them.

I looked under their feet for the Yaqui. I called his name. He did not answer. At last I saw his track and followed. I called again. Then out of a hole in the snow came the Yaqui's head. He blinked in the dim sunlight, then leaped upon me. He squeezed me.

"You are not dead! You are not dead!" he whispered. "The

JUAN, THE YAQUI

Sky Father saved you. The Earth Mother not let you sleep. You not sleep in storm and freeze! You find camp. I no could kill you, *amigo*. I no could kill a lamb with broken leg."

He took a bit of the sacred meal from the buckskin bag at his belt and tossed it to the six directions. Then he crept back into the hole in the snow. I followed. It was warm there.

"How did you not die in the storm?" I asked, as we lay close in the warm earth.

"I must keep sheep," he answered. "Your father's sheep. And you not dead. Your mother not say, 'Juan de los Yaquis let die my son.' Now I sleep."

The boy had bunched the sheep and kept them turning while the snow drifted a wall about them. He had pulled limbs from the spruce for their food. He had dug deep into a gravelly spot, filled it with wood, and built a fire. When the ground was warm on all sides, he had let the fire die. On the ashes were branches of spruce. Spruce covered the top. The drifting snow kept out the wind. Juan needed no sheepskins to keep warm.

The next day we drove the flock down the mountain. When we reached camp the Yaqui took from his buckskin bag a handful of small, yellow stones. They shone in the sunset.

"They were under me in the gravel," he said, dropping them into my hand. "No more I dig in deep holes for yellow sand. I be your brother. We herd our father's sheep."

Young Mountainy Singer

By Martha F. Simmonds

LEE BURNEY and his sister Barbara lay on the bearskin in front of the fireplace. They were watching the bright flames eat away the logs, and talking in low tones. As a moan came from the bunk in the dark corner of the cabin, they were silent. Then, softly, they began to talk again.

"I reckon we won't get to go to the singin' at the schoolhouse," Lee whispered wistfully. "I sure craved to hear the ballads and all the mountainy songs."

"Don't think of a singin', with Pappy layin' there sufferin' so," Barbara reproached him. "Anyhow, it's a long time yet, an' maybe he'll be well."

"Yes, if Pappy'd be better so we could leave," Lee said, "maybe the neighbors would come this way an' take us to the singin'. You know Mom wouldn't let us go alone after dark."

"No, not when we have to climb up out of this valley. It'd be

94

a mournful thing to miss a gatherin', though, an' a sight harder to miss it in winter, when we're shut in so."

"Seems like I'll just have to hear that singin'," Lee looked at his sister wistfully, "I'd rather be a mountainy singer than *anything*."

"Rather than bein' best wrestler in Deep Hollow?" asked Barbara in surprise.

"Yes."

"Or the best shot in the hills?"

"Rather than anything."

Barbara looked at him solemnly. "Well, effen you ever mean to try to be a singer, you better begin to learn."

"I know a lot of mountainy songs," he whispered. "Sometimes I sing, when I'm on the high path alone, or when Pappy sends me to Stice's. But I sing soft, so nobody'll hear me."

"Why soft, Lee? Why don't you sing loud?"

"I don't want 'em to hear. They'd laugh. 'Tain't for a youngun to be a mountainy singer. That's fer men."

A soft footfall came across the cabin. Their mother stood there, with deep trouble in her face.

"Yore pappy's worse," she said, "and there's a ways you must go, quick before night comes over the mountain. You climb the mountain to the Lookout Point an' then go over Painted Rock way to Miller's. That's shortest. Ask 'em would they get word for help. They'll know what to do. An' mind you hurry as smart as you can, fer Pappy's that bad!"

"May we take the dogs, Mom?"

"No, ye've no call to need them. There's daylight enough to get there. You could stay the night if you need, or come with them. I'm thinkin' some one'll trudge down to my help, come night."

She saw them out the door and stood on the step, watching. They were sturdy enough, those two, and used to climbing; they would make it safely. She should have sent them last night, when their father had crawled in from the wood lot; or this morning. But mountain folk do not easily ask for help, and she had waited, thinking to get along all right by herself.

Up the steep path Lee and Barbara clambered, with no words. Climbing brought warmth in spite of the chill air. Higher and higher they went, until to their mother, who came out on the step again and shaded her eyes to look at them, they were but tiny moving dots.

They reached Lookout Point and started over Painted Rock way. It was a narrow path, steeply and crazily bending around the side of the mountain. It seemed a bit slippery today, and the wind blew coldly through their clothes and took their breath when they made the sudden turns.

All at once, as she rounded a corner, Barbara felt the rock she leaned against give way. It came down all about her, startlingly. She was a true mountain girl and did not even scream, but Lee, ahead, heard the noise.

"Barb'ry?" he called, almost before he turned to look. She stood there, as the loosened earth and rocks tumbled on down

the mountainside.

"You hurt?"

"No, I don't feel so."

He came close. "Then come. Let's get over this stretch."

Barbara started, and then realized that she could not. "Lee, my foot's caught."

"Can't you pull it out?"

She tugged. "No, I can't."

"There doesn't look to be much rock there holding it."

"I think it's in a crack like, Lee. It's slipped sideways."

"I'll shove against the rock an' you pull on your foot."

It was no use. Lee looked at the top of Barbara's shoe where it disappeared beneath the edge of the fallen rock.

"There's loose dirt an' stone there. Maybe I can dig some away, an' make room."

He knelt down and tried with his hands to dig, but after a few handfuls, he struck the rock of the path. He could see her foot better, though. It was wedged tightly in a crack of the rock, with the fallen stones over it. He tugged at those and finally got them all

97

out of the way but one—the last heavy one. He stood back to get his breath.

"It's—gettin' dark, Lee."

He looked at the sky. The long-expected snow was coming! Dark clouds seemed to be climbing out of nowhere.

"Is it—is it late yet?"

"No, Barb'ry." He answered briefly, but his voice was serious. Late or not, when the black dark of a moonless night came over the mountain, it was not a safe place for a boy and a girl alone, without even a dog! Barbara was shaking.

"Cold?" Lee asked.

She nodded. They were on the place in all the mountain where the wind blew fiercest and the cold bit most deeply into them.

"You—maybe you better go on, Lee."

"I can't, Barb'ry. I can't get there soon enough."

"What'll we do? If we just had a dog!"

"I'd rather have that old crowbar down by the shed," Lee said, "I could pry with it."

He looked around. Unmistakably, it was darker.

"Mom never thought it'd darken so soon," Barbara said mournfully. "An' she couldn't dream I'd get caught like this."

"I tell you," Lee suggested, "let's unlace your shoe far as we can, an' see if you can pull your foot out, an' then get the shoe out."

Quickly he dropped down to the path, pulled off his mittens and unfastened the laces. Barbara tried to pull out her foot.

"I can move it better," she cried excitedly.

"Tip it a little toward the rock," Lee said. "Now I'm goin' to brace myself on the path an' put my shoulders against the big rock. An' when I say the word, I'll push hard as I can an' you tip and twist an' pull your foot. We got to get out o' here, Barb'ry. I can't leave you, and I've got nothin' but my hands to protect you with."

"I know," she answered fearfully, through chattering teeth.

"All ready—now!" He pushed with all his might and Barbara tugged and twisted. Just when it seemed to Lee that his back would break, Barbara cried out, "It's loose!" and clutched at him to keep from going over the side of the mountain.

With her foot out, the shoe could be released easily. Lee tried to rub her numb foot, and when the prickles began to sting like needles, she put it into the shoe. At the first step, however, she winced, and tears filled her eyes. "It hurts. I guess I twisted it to a sprain."

Lee was standing up, drawing on his mittens. "You lean on me," he said manfully. "We've got to hurry."

"I know." She shut her mouth against the pain, but tears dripped down her cheeks as she hobbled around the turn, along the rest of the narrow grade, and reached the wider path.

"Miller's is nearest, Barb'ry, an' I don't dare leave you."

"No, course you don't." She looked ahead where the woods loomed. There was a level stretch there, as nearly level, that is, as any part of the mountains. For nearly half a mile they trudged through the piney woods, and night was coming fast.

By the time they reached the edge of the trees, they could scarcely see one another. Lee stopped. "I've got my knife, an' I'll cut a big piney knot an' light it."

"What'll you light it with?"

"I've got store matches in my pocket," he said proudly. "The three matches Pappy give me last summer, I've still got."

He cut the piney knot. Beside a big tree trunk, Barbara spread her dress wide and held her scarf out and Lee crouched in the

shelter. The first match did not light the wood. The head of the second flew off and was gone. Very, very carefully he lit the third, and the pine caught, and held.

"You just hold that until I get another."

They were in the center of the woods before they heard the sound for which each had listened fearfully. Long and keen and quivering, it cut the air like a knife and howled mournfully in the pines. Wolves! Barbara tried to hurry, and Lee held the torch higher. But the cry came again, and there was an answer.

"Help me up in a tree, Lee, an' you go on. Go to Miller's an' come back."

"I can't do that, Barb'ry. It'd take too long with your lame ankle. An' you're that cold to be hangin' in a tree with—with—Anyhow, I won't do it."

A little farther, and the light of the pine knot picked out in the darkness two shining circles of light. A little farther back, Lee saw two others.

"Stop, Lee!" cried Barbara. "Oh, we can't go on! What'll we do? We can't turn back either."

He held the lighted torch in his right hand, as far in front as he could, and he started to light the

other one. No—better wait—he might need a light a long time.

"Lee, we ought to make a noise—but I—I can hardly talk!"

Lee burst out into a rollicking tune:

> "She'll be comin' round the mountain when she comes—
> She'll be comin' round the mountain when she comes—"

He had not dreamed he could sing so loud. He advanced a step —another—and the eyes ahead of him retreated ever so slightly. Barbara clung to his arm and followed.

Singing lustily, he inched his way along. He dared not look back or to the side, yet he dared not hurry. If there were other eyes watching from behind and he seemed to run, the wolves would rush in! He held the light higher, sang louder, and went on steadily. His heart sank, when he noticed that the wind blew away from the Miller's cabin!

Lee could not know that up along the Devil's Backbone, Tom Hogan was striding home with his gun and his dog. A stray and freakish current of wind carried a sound.

"She'll be drivin' six white horses when she comes"—

It was a youngun—singin'—on a night like this. That must mean trouble, for it was not a natural thing to hear. What could be wrong? But the dog had caught something in the wind. He stopped. The hair on his neck rose in straight, stiff bristles and he growled.

"Wolves, Lightnin'? Let's git down thar!"

The man seemed to fling himself over the mountainside. And with him went the dog. Tom Hogan shot his gun resoundingly into the air, and the dog bayed deeply. And then Lee and Barbara could no longer see the eyes ahead of them. Although she was a girl of the hills, Barbara began to shake all over and to sob. Lee walked faster, but he kept his torch flaring and he kept singing until he heard a voice shout:

"Youngun! Where you be?"

Lee cried out, "Here!" and in a few minutes something touched his hand—the cold, friendly nose of a great hound. Then a tall figure loomed up out of the trees.

The story was soon told to the newcomer. Tom Hogan handed Lee his gun.

"Reckon you kin pack that? It's a man's gun, but you've shown yourself a man tonight." At that, Lee's heart swelled with happiness. Tom Hogan put Barbara on his back and made quick work of the rest of the woods.

A few more minutes and they were inside Miller's cabin. But when Lee tried to tell his story, his throat was so sore and his voice so hoarse, he faltered. He could hardly speak, and Barbara had to explain for him. As soon as the Millers understood what had hap-

pened, they were making ready to
go to the Burney cabin and help
take care of Lee's sick father.

"We'll git help to your pappy.
He'll be all right."

Tom Hogan looked at Lee
and Barbara. "These younguns
better spend the night here, I
reckon."

"Grandma'll fix Barb'ry's
ankle," said the younger mountain woman, as she drew on her
heavy overshoes.

And then Tom Hogan
grinned.

"And while you're workin',
Grandma, wrap up the neck of
this mountainy singer in some
good hot grease. We'll want his
voice at the singin' an' I reckon
he's sung it just about out," he
said, as he picked up his gun to go
up the mountain with his friends,
the Millers.

Lee looked at Barbara. They'd
get to go to the singin'! Then he
realized that Tom Hogan—a man
of the hills—had called him a
mountainy singer. It was the hap-
piest moment of his life.

JOYCE BALLANTYNE

Locked in

By Elizabeth Enright

I T HAD BEEN one of those dull, dull days when nothing
interesting happens and everything goes wrong. It was the
kind of day that you stub your toe a lot and lose things, and
forget what it was your mother asked you to get at the store.
Garnet kept swallowing great, hollow yawns and wishing that
something would happen: an earthquake, or an escaped hyena
from a circus. Anything!

"I know what," she said to her chum, Citronella, "Let's go to
town to the library and read. It's still early."

Citronella objected for a minute or two, because she said she
didn't feel like walking all the way to Blaiseville. But Garnet was
sure they could get a ride with someone, and soon persuaded her
to come.

As luck would have it, the moment they went out they saw Mr.
Freebody's truck clattering down the road towards them. They
waved and called, and Mr. Freebody stopped and opened the door

to let them in. He was going to town to buy feed.

"We'd rather ride outside, if you don't mind," said Garnet, and the two girls scrambled into the back of the truck and stood up, holding onto the roof over the driver's seat.

It was fun to ride like that, because as soon as he got on the highway Mr. Freebody drove fast. The wind blew so hard against them that Garnet's pigtails stuck straight out behind, and Citronella's bang stood up on end like a hedge. They felt as though their noses were blown flat against their faces, and when they spoke their words flew away from them.

"I feel like a thing on the front of a boat," shouted Garnet. "A figurehead, I think it's called."

Citronella had never heard of figureheads. They watched the truck swallow up the flat ribbon of road like a tape measure; the little gray town of Blaiseville flew towards them. There it was, all just as usual: the courthouse with its tower, the gasoline station, and the red painted depot. There was Opal Clyde, the doctor's daughter, bouncing a ball on the walk in front of her house, and there was Junior Gertz pulling his dog along in a little express wagon. Garnet and Citronella waved as they rode grandly by. Mr. Freebody drew up in front of the Farm Bureau; and the girls jumped down.

"How you two girls going to git home?" asked Mr. Freebody.

"Oh, we'll walk, maybe," answered Garnet. "Or get a ride with someone," added Citronella hopefully.

They thanked him and walked up the Main Street past the blacksmith's and the drugstore and the post office. There was a bulletin in the post-office window that said: "Big Hollow Ladies Annual Picnic Next Sunday. Come One, Come All!" Garnet giggled at this notice, seeing in her mind a group of huge balloon-like creatures in dresses eating sandwiches under a tree. Of course she knew that the Big Hollow Ladies were simply ladies that lived in Big Hollow, but it had a funny sound all the same. They went on up the street past the store full of straw hats and overalls, and the shoe store.

Finally on the outskirts of the town they came to the library, an old-fashioned building set back from the road among thick-foilaged maple trees. Garnet loved the library; it smelled deliciously of old books and was full of stories that she had never read. Miss Pentland, the librarian, was a nice fat lady who sat behind an enormous desk facing the door.

"Good afternoon, Citronella," she said, smiling. "Good afternoon, Ruby."

Miss Pentland always called Garnet Ruby by mistake. There were so many little girls in Blaiseville with names like jewels that it was very confusing. There were Ruby Schwarz, Ruby Harvey, and Rubye Smalley; Pearl Orison and Pearl Schoenbecker; Beryl Schultz, and little Opal Clyde.

Garnet and Citronella poked about among the books until each had found the one she wanted. Then they settled down on a broad window seat between two tall cases of large old volumes.

Garnet had *The Jungle Book*, and Citronella with a sigh of pleasure began to read a wonderful story called *Duchess Olga: or The Sapphire Signet*.

Many times the screen door creaked and closed with a muffled bang as people came and went; other children and grown people, old ladies looking for books on crocheting, and boys wanting stories about G-men. For a while rain splintered against the window, but they scarcely heard it. Garnet was thousands of miles away with Kotick, the white seal, swimming the wide seas to find a safe island for his people. And Citronella was in a ballroom lighted by a hundred chandeliers and crowded with beautiful ladies and gentlemen in full evening dress.

Garnet finished "The White Seal" and went on to "Toomai of the Elephants." Once she looked up and stretched. "My, it's quiet," she whispered. "I wonder if it's late."

"Oh, we haven't been here long," said Citronella. She had reached the most exciting part of the book, where Duchess Olga was being lowered on a rope down the face of a huge cliff. The man who held the rope didn't like Duchess Olga and was planning to let her drop at any minute. Citronella thought everything would turn out all right, but she wasn't sure.

By the time that Garnet had re-read "Rikki-Tikki-Tavi," and Duchess Olga had been rescued pages back and safely returned to the ballroom, the light began to fade.

"What does the word 'insidious' mean?" asked Citronella, but Garnet didn't know.

"My, it is kind of still," she went on. "I'll ask Miss Pentland what time it is." She disappeared behind the bookcases.

"Garnet!" she called loudly the next moment. "Miss Pentland's gone! Everyone's gone!"

Garnet leaped from the window seat. It was true; there was no one there. They ran to the door, but it was locked. The back door was locked too; and the heavy glass windows had not been opened in years. It was impossible to move them.

"Good night!" moaned Citronella. "We're locked in!" She was on the verge of tears.

But Garnet felt pleasantly excited.

"Citronella," she said solemnly, "this is an adventure. We'll be able to tell our children and grandchildren about it. I hope we stay here all night!"

"Oh gee," sobbed Citronella. She wished with all her heart that she hadn't read *Duchess Olga;* it was too scary. If only she had picked out a book about boarding-school girls or something, she wouldn't be so frightened now. Suddenly she had such a terrible thought that she stopped crying.

"Garnet!" she cried. "Do you know what day it is? Saturday! That means we'll be here till day after tomorrow. We'll starve!"

Garnet's excitement went flat. It would be awful to stay in here as long as that. "Let's bang on the windows," she suggested. "Maybe someone will come."

They banged on the glass and shouted at the tops of their lungs. But the library was some distance from the street, and the thick maples deadened the noise they made. Blaiseville people were eating their suppers and never heard a sound.

Slowly the dusk sifted into the room. The bookcases looked tall and solemn, and the pictures on the wall were solemn, too: steel engravings of "Napoleon at Elba," and "Washington

LOCKED IN

Crossing the Delaware."

There was no telephone in the library and no electric light. There were gas fixtures, but Garnet and Citronella could not find any matches. They rummaged through Miss Pentland's desk, but it was full of useless things like filing cards, rubber stamps, elastic bands, and neat rolls of string.

Citronella pounced upon a chocolate bar in a pigeonhole.

"We won't starve anyhow," she said. "I don't think Miss Pentland would mind if we ate it, do you?"

"We'll buy her another," said Garnet; so they divided it and stood, sadly munching, at the window nearest the street.

"Who is that!" cried Garnet suddenly. They saw a dim, small figure slowly approaching on the cement walk that led to the library door. The person seemed to be bowing.

Citronella began thumping on the window. "It's Opal Clyde, bouncing her ball," she said. "Yell, Garnet. Yell and bang."

They both yelled and banged; Opal, after a scared glance at the dark window, scurried down the path as fast as she could go.

"Do you think she'll tell someone?" asked Citronella.

"Oh, she thought it was a spook," said Garnet in disgust. "Probably no one will believe her if she does."

All over Blaiseville the street lamps blossomed suddenly with light, but only a faint gleam penetrated the maple leaves. The two girls heard cars coming and going, and they pounded and called till they were hoarse. But nobody came.

After a while they gave it up as a bad job and returned to the window seat.

The room was very dark now: strange, unknown, and filled with shadows. There were tiny creaking sounds and rustlings and airy scamperings of mouse feet.

"I don't like it," whispered Citronella. "I don't like it at all. My own voice scares me. I don't dare talk out loud."

"Neither do I," murmured Garnet. "I feel as if all those books were alive and listening."

"I wonder why our folks don't come," said Citronella.

"They don't even know we came to town, and we didn't tell Mr. Freebody that we were going to the library."

"I wish I'd never learned to read," sighed Citronella. "I wish I was some kind of animal and didn't have to be educated."

"It might be fun to be a panther," agreed Garnet, "or a kangaroo, or a monkey."

"Or a pig even," said Citronella. "A safe, happy pig asleep in its own pen with its own family!"

"One that had never seen a library and couldn't even spell pork," added Garnet, and giggled. Citronella giggled too, and they both felt much better.

Outside the night wind stirred among the trees, and a maple scratched at the window glass with a tiny finger. But inside it was close and still except for the small mysterious sounds that can be heard in all old houses after dark.

Garnet and Citronella huddled together and whispered. They heard the courthouse clock strike eight, then nine; but when it struck ten they were both sound asleep.

At a little before midnight they were wakened by a tremendous pounding and shouting.

"Who? What's that? Where am I?" shrieked Citronella in a panic. Garnet, her heart thumping, said, "In the library, remember? Someone's at the door."

She ran forward in the dark, barking her shins and whacking her elbows on unfamiliar surfaces.

"Who's there?" she called.

"That you, Garnet? Thank the Lord we've found you at last," said a voice that was unmistakably Mr. Freebody's. "Is Citronella with you? Fine! Both your dads are scouring the town for you. Open the door!"

"But we're locked *in*, Mr. Freebody," called Garnet. "Miss Pentland has the key."

"I'll get it. I'll get it," shouted Mr. Freebody excitedly. "You wait there."

"We can't do anything *but* wait," said Citronella crossly. She was always cross when she first woke up.

In a little while they heard rapid footsteps on the front walk, and voices, and then the lovely sound of a key turning in the lock. Miss Pentland, with her hat on sideways, rushed in.

"You poor little things!" she cried. "Such a thing has *never* happened before; I always make sure everyone's gone before I lock up. I can't understand how I missed you!"

"That's all right, Miss Pentland," said Garnet. "It was an adventure. And we ate your chocolate!"

Garnet's father and Mr. Freebody and Mr. Hauser came in too.

"Are you both sure you're all right?" asked Mr. Hauser, his fat, kind face looking pale for the first time in years.

"We're all right, Papa," said Citronella. "But we're awfully hungry."

"I'll go telephone the folks at home," volunteered Mr. Freebody. "So's they won't have to worry no longer. You better take the little girls down to the lunch wagon for a bite. Only place that's open at this hour."

The lunch wagon was down by the railroad tracks; neither Garnet nor Citronella had ever been there before. It was full of bright yellow light, and cigar smoke and powerful food smells. It was wonderful to go there so late at night and eat fried egg sandwiches and apple pie and tell everybody what had happened.

"Yes, sir!" said Mr. Freebody, coming to the door. "Don't you be fooled! Those ain't two little girls you see settin' up there; those are two genuwine bookworms, couldn't stop reading long enough to come home."

Everyone laughed.

"Just the same," whispered Garnet to Citronella, "I sort of wish they hadn't found us until morning. Then we could have told our grandchildren that once we stayed in the public library all night long!"

From *Thimble Summer*

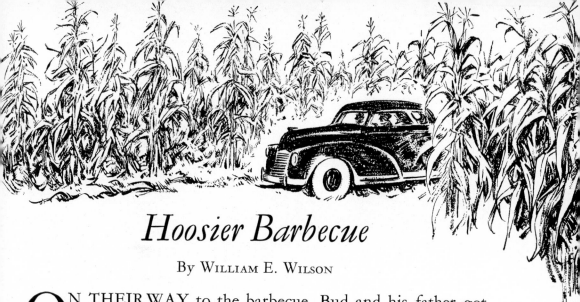

Hoosier Barbecue

By William E. Wilson

ON THEIR WAY to the barbecue, Bud and his father got lost. "Well, son, I haven't any idea where we are! But these are the bottoms all right, and the picnic ground must be around somewhere. Corn doesn't grow as high as this anywhere except in the bottom lands."

"What'll we do, Dad?" asked Bud.

"There's nothing to do but to keep going till we find a road that looks promising," answered his father.

They drove on, and the road narrowed and grew lonelier. They saw no one. From time to time there was a tumble-down corncrib made of poles, or a tool shed, or an old rusty piece of farm machinery; but there was no other sign of life. There was nothing but the tall corn and hot, bright sunshine.

They drove perhaps five miles through the unchanging corn-land, until the road ended abruptly on a bluff overhanging the Wabash River. Bud's father whistled as he jammed on the brakes. Bud looked down over the bluff and caught his breath. The river was fifty feet or more below them. Far away he saw a solitary man fishing from a boat. "Why did they ever build a road right to the edge like this?" he asked.

"They didn't," his father said, wiping the sweat from his face with his handkerchief. "Last spring the river came up and bit off a piece of the land. That's why the corn grows right to the edge of the bluff, too. The land caved into the river after the corn

was planted."

They tried another fork in the dusty, unused road, and then another and another. Finally they struck a gravel road. Then Bud saw his father relax over the wheel. Soon they were climbing a low hill that rose like an island in the sea of cornland—a little island of green grass and cottonwood trees.

"Here we are!" Bud's father said; and they parked the car among the others that were already there and climbed out.

"Well, if it isn't Bud and his pa!" called Bud's grandpa, who was picking his way toward them among the cars. "We'd just about given you up!"

Bud liked his grandpa. He liked the way he was always hitching up the faded blue shoulder straps of his overalls. He liked the way his grandpa's white mustache curled at the ends. He liked the way grandpa talked too—that excited, exaggerated, joking way.

"We got lost," Bud said.

"Lost, eh?" Grandpa laughed and slapped his thighs with his gnarled brown hands. "Well, I'm not surprised! They tell me there's city fellers still wandering around in the bottom lands today that came down ten years ago to shoot ducks!"

Then suddenly he grew serious, and, taking in the country-

side with a sweep of his arm, began to talk as if he were address-
ing a group of strangers instead
of his own son and grandson.

"Now, this is right in the
heart of the bottoms, where the
Wabash and Ohio rivers meet. There is a gravel road all the way
down here, but I guess you missed it. This land is all under water every spring, and in the big flood of 'thirty-seven the water
came up over the top of this hill. Yes, sir!

"This is an Indian mound you see. It isn't natural. It was
made a thousand years ago by the Mound Builders. They buried
their dead in it. Your pa and his brothers used to find thigh bones
and arrowheads and teapots here when they were young. They
tell me you have to dig down only a foot or two."

He stopped, then turned to Bud and his father. "But why am
I standing here gabbing when you two must be half starved?
Come on! Let's get going to the barbecue! It's right over there
on that other mound. This one's just for parking cars."

As they started down into the hollow that separated the two
mounds, he gave Bud's hair a tug.

"Barbecue, Bud! Good old-fashioned hickory barbecue! Beef,
mutton, and pork! You can take your pick—or a double helping
of each! And enough pie and cake to feed every man, woman,
and child in Posey County! Owmm!"

As Bud listened, he felt the emptiness of his stomach grow

emptier, and he started down through the hollow at a run. Half-way to the second Indian mound, the first whiff of the barbecue smoke reached his nose. It was a compound of fragrant hickory, juicy roasting meat, and spicy sauces that made him weak with hunger. He and his father and Grandpa leaped the narrow creek at the bottom of the hollow in one bound, and climbed the hill on the other side. All the farmers and farmers' wives and children of Hooppole Township seemed to be on top of the hill, eating and laughing.

Bud made straight for the barbecue pit and stood there a moment, watching. Heavy wire screens held whole sheep and pigs and beeves over the hickory fire in the pit, and men stood by constantly swabbing the meat with long poles which they dipped in a great sauce kettle. But Bud did not stay long. In another minute he was holding out his plate to the man who was carving and serving.

"Some of each," Bud said.

The man forked up large slabs of the crisp meat—one of beef, one of pork, and one of mutton—and placed them between two slices of rye bread with pickle and onion. Then he poured several spoonfuls of brown sauce over the sandwich.

As he took the plate Bud licked his lips, and the man grinned at him. "Come back for more, son, when that's gone!"

From the barbecue pit, Bud moved to the tables where the rest of the food was served. The tables were wide boards set up on sawhorses, and they sagged with the weight of the food piled on them. There were yellow mountains of steaming ears of corn and blocks of rich butter. There were potato salads and deviled eggs and ham and cold fried chicken. There were pies—apple, blackberry, gooseberry, chocolate, and lemon. And cakes of three and even four layers, with chocolate, lemon, and strawberry icing almost as thick as the cake itself. And, of course, there was ice cream and hot coffee and bottles of cold pop and red lemonade.

Bud loaded his plate and then came back for more.

"Just help yourself, son! Here, try some of this devil's food cake too!"

"Don't be shy! Step right up and take what you want! Did you get some of the barbecued spareribs?"

He ate some of everything and a great deal of some things; then his grandpa came up with a third helping of ice cream.

"How about the southeast corner of the northwest section of your stomach, Bud? You've got room in there for this, haven't you?" he asked; and Bud nodded.

But Bud was wrong. He had to leave half the ice cream in the dish. It was the first time in his life that such a thing had happened to him.

By the time he was through, the crowd was already moving away from the barbecue pit and the tables, to gather around a speakers' stand. Here the Governor of Indiana and some other important people were waiting to be introduced. Bud took a good look at the Governor from the branches of a poplar tree, and then sauntered off. He decided to skip the speechmaking, for a plan had formed in his mind. Ever since he had swallowed his last possible bite of ice cream, he had been remembering something his grandpa said.

"You have to dig down only a foot or two—!"

"An Indian mound—thigh bones—arrowhead—teapots!"

Bud made sure that his father and grandpa were busy listening to the speakers. Then he darted down into the hollow and across the creek to the mound where the cars were parked.

There was a ramshackle shed on the Indian mound, and in it Bud found what he wanted—a spade. He stayed for several minutes in the shed, examining a rowboat and some fishing tackle stored there and listening to the drone of insects. When he had

looked everything over, he went
out and began to dig.

"If any of those kids come
over here," he said to himself,
"I'll just tell 'em I'm digging for fishing worms."

The earth was dry and hard and dusty; and although he worked
in the shade, he was very hot. He dug and dug, making trenches
and pits and circular holes; but all he found was a piece of rotten
harness strap, a tin can or two, and a dog's bone.

"Arrowheads and teapots!" he thought disgustedly. Maybe
his grandpa was only joking again.

Because he was bending over at his work, Bud did not see
the change coming over the sky; and when the first drop of rain
fell, it startled him. Immediately after it came another—and another. He looked up. The sky, which had been such a dazzling
blue, was an angry yellow now and growing darker. Bud gazed
across the hollow at the picnic grounds, debating whether or not
to run for it and join his father and grandpa. But the rain decided
for him. It came all at once, not in drops but in pailfuls, accom-
panied by a crash of thunder. He brushed his soaked hair out of
his eyes and ran blindly toward the shed through the almost
solid wall of water.

"It's a cloudburst!" he
panted, shaking himself when he
was inside the shed. "It's a real
cloudburst."

He sat down in the stern of the rowboat and tried to wring
the water out of his shirt, but the effort was wasted. In a few
minutes rain was leaking through the roof in little showers. It
was dark in the shed, and through the sheet of water that slanted
across the doorway Bud could see nothing.

The rain lasted twenty minutes. Then it stopped as suddenly
as it had begun. Bud stepped out of the shed. The air was so fresh
and clean he could taste it. The dust had been washed from the
grass and cottonwoods, and the world was painted a new green.
In the parking lot, the cars sparkled brightly.

"Boy!" Bud said. "I'll bet the barbecue got soaked!"

He walked around the shed to look across the hollow and
was stopped short.

The hollow was gone! Between him and the picnic ground,
instead, stretched a wide expanse of brown water. He stood still
with his mouth open, staring. He could not believe that the little
creek could have grown to a river in less than a half hour. But it
had. And there, on the picnic ground, the people were staring
helplessly at the brown flood.

Suddenly it came to Bud how helpless they were. From his own Indian mound, the road was still above water and passable. But from their Indian mound there was no road. They were no longer on a mound. They were on an island. They were completely surrounded by water, with no means of escape. Bud's eyes widened. His mouth fell open.

"Goodness!" he said aloud. "They're marooned!"

Then he began to yell, "Hello! Dad! Grandpa! Hello!"

When they saw him, they began to yell. He could not understand what they were saying. He could only see them jumping up and down, waving their arms. Even the Governor was waving.

For a long time they waved and yelled at each other: Bud alone on his Indian mound where the cars were parked, the picknickers huddled together on theirs where the barbecue had been. And all the while the sirupy brown water flowed swiftly between them. Finally, Bud realized he would have to go and get help. He turned and walked back around the shed.

It was then that fear hit him for the first time—right in the middle of his stomach. He remembered the tall corn of the bottom lands and the winding roads. If he left his Indian mound and went down into the bottom lands in search of help, he would surely get lost. He began to shiver, for his wet shirt was now cold on his back and his mind was suddenly filled with a hundred crowding fears. It would be growing dark in a few hours. He could not reach his father, and his father could not reach him. He would have to spend the night alone where the Mound Builders used to bury their dead.

At that moment his eye fell on the rowboat in the shed. At once all his fears were turned into the strength of a single purpose and action.

It was no easy task to drag the rowboat out across the rain-soaked earth—pulling, shoving, straining. And, once on the water, the rowing was the hardest he had ever done. Eddies and currents tugged and poked the prow, so that half the time, it seemed to him, he was rowing in the wrong direction. But he was not a Hoosier boy for nothing. He was at home in a rowboat. He knew the tricks of flood currents and whirlpools. His arms were strong. And when he was halfway across, he had the cheers of the picnickers to encourage him.

Still, it seemed to take forever to get across the water. His arms ached. His hands were sore. His head grew dizzy.

But at last he made it.

In the excitement that followed his landing, the people almost overlooked him. They patted him on the head, of course, and a half dozen women kissed him before he could escape. But the farmers were feeling so troubled about the Governor, who was soaked to the skin, that they set to work at once rowing him across to the parking space.

After that, the rescue work progressed rapidly. Some of the men went home and brought back their own boats to put into service. At last all the picnickers were safely ferried across the swollen creek and on their way home in their cars.

Bud and his father crossed on the last trip—because Grandpa was on the barbecue committee and felt he had to stay "till the last feller's ashore," as he put it. By the time they reached the parking lot and climbed into their car, Bud was dead tired. His arms and legs ached. His eyes were heavy.

"Bud, I want to tell you how proud I am of you," Grandpa was saying. "You did a dangerous thing, a-bringin' that boat across the flood—and a brave thing. You acted like a man!"

But Bud did not hear his grandpa's words of praise. He was sound asleep on his father's shoulder—and dreaming of thigh bones and teapots and arrowheads.

From *High Road to Glory*

The Sugar Snow

THE STORY OF A PIONEER FAMILY
By Laura Ingalls Wilder

FOR days the sun shone and the weather was warm. There was no frost on the windows in the mornings. All day the icicles fell one by one from the eaves, with soft smashing and crackling sounds. The trees shook their wet, black branches, and chunks of snow fell down.

When Mary and Laura pressed their noses against the cold windowpane they could see the drip of water from the eaves. The snow did not glitter; it looked soft and tired. Under the trees it was pitted where the chunks of snow had fallen, and the banks beside the path were shrinking and settling.

Then one day Laura saw a patch of bare ground in the yard. All day it grew bigger, and before night the whole yard was bare mud. Only the icy path was left, and the snowbanks along the path and the fence and beside the woodpile.

"May I go out to play?" she asked.

"You may tomorrow," Ma promised.

That night Laura woke up, shivering. The bedcovers felt thin, and her nose was icy cold. Ma was tucking another quilt over her.

"Snuggle close to Mary," Ma said, "and you'll get warm."

In the morning the house was warm from the stove, but when Laura looked out of the window she saw that the ground was covered with soft, thick snow. All along the branches of the trees the snow was piled like feathers, and it lay in mounds along the top of the rail fence, and stood up in great, white balls on top of the gateposts.

Pa came in, shaking the soft snow from his shoulders and stamping it from his boots.

THE SUGAR SNOW

"It's a sugar snow," he said.

Laura put her tongue to a bit of the white snow that lay in a fold of his sleeve. It was nothing but wet on her tongue, like any snow. She was glad that nobody had seen her taste it.

"Why is it a sugar snow, Pa?" she asked him, but he said he didn't have time to explain now. He must hurry away; he was going to Grandpa's.

Grandpa lived far away in the Big Woods, where the trees were close together and larger.

Laura stood at the window and watched Pa, big and swift and strong, walking away over the snow. His gun was on his shoulder; his hatchet and powder horn hung at his side, and his tall boots made great tracks in the soft snow. Laura watched him till he was out of sight in the woods.

It was late before he came home. Ma had lighted the lamp when he came in. Under one arm he carried a large package, and in the other hand was a big, covered, wooden bucket.

"Here, Caroline," he said, handing the package and the bucket to Ma. Then he put the gun on its hooks over the door.

"If I'd met a bear," he said, "I couldn't have shot him without dropping my load." He laughed. "And if I'd dropped that bucket and bundle, I wouldn't have had to shoot him. I could have watched him eat what's in them and lick his chops."

Ma unwrapped the package and there were two hard, brown cakes, each as large as a milk pan. She uncovered the bucket, and it was full of dark brown sirup.

"Here, Laura and Mary," Pa said, and he gave them each a little round package out of his pocket.

They took off the paper wrappings, and each had a little, hard, brown cake, with beautifully crinkled edges.

"Bite it," said Pa, and his blue eyes twinkled.

Each bit off one little crinkle, and it was sweet. It crumbled in their mouths. It was better than their Christmas candy.

"Maple sugar," said Pa.

Supper was ready, and Laura and Mary laid the little maple sugar cakes beside their plates, while they ate the maple sirup on their bread.

After supper, Pa took them on his knees before the fire, and told them about his day at Grandpa's, and the sugar snow.

"All winter," Pa said, "Grandpa has been making wooden buckets and little troughs. He made them of cedar and white ash, for those woods won't give a bad taste to the maple sirup.

"To make the troughs, he split out sticks as long as my hand and as big as my two fingers. Near one end, Grandpa cut the stick half through, and split one half off. This left a flat stick, with a square piece at one end. With a bit he bored a hole lengthwise through the square part. With his knife he whittled the wood till it was only a thin shell around the hole. The flat part of the stick he hollowed out with his knife till it was a little trough.

"He made dozens of them, and he made ten new wooden buckets. He had them all ready when the first warm weather came and the sap began to move in the trees.

THE SUGAR SNOW

"Then he went into the maple woods and with the bit he bored a hole in each maple tree, and he hammered the round end of the little trough into the hole, and he set a cedar bucket on the ground under the flat end.

"The sap, you know, is the blood of a tree. It comes up from the roots in the spring, and it goes to the very tip of each branch and twig, to make the green leaves grow.

"Well, when the maple sap came to the hole in the tree, it ran out of the tree, down the trough, and into the bucket."

"Oh, didn't it hurt the poor tree?" Laura asked.

"No more than it hurts you when you prick your finger and it bleeds," said Pa.

"Every day Grandpa goes out into the snowy woods and gathers the sap. With a barrel on a sled, he drives from tree to tree and empties the sap from the buckets into the barrel. Then he hauls it to a big iron kettle that hangs by a chain from a cross timber between two trees.

"He empties the sap into the iron kettle. There is a big bonfire under the kettle, and the sap boils, and Grandpa watches it carefully. The fire must be hot enough to keep the sap boiling, but not hot enough to make it boil over.

"Every few minutes the sap must be skimmed. Grandpa skims it with a big, long-handled, wooden ladle that he made of basswood. When the sap gets too hot, Grandpa lifts ladlefuls of it high in the air and pours it back slowly. This cools the sap a little and keeps it from boiling too fast.

"When the sap has boiled down just enough, he fills the buckets with the sirup. After that, he boils

the sap until it grains when he cools it in a saucer.

"The instant the sap is graining, Grandpa jumps to the fire and rakes it all out from beneath the kettle. Then, as fast as he can he ladles the thick sirup into the milk pans that are standing ready. In the pans the sirup turns to cakes of hard, brown, maple sugar."

"So that's why it's a sugar snow, because Grandpa is making sugar?" Laura asked.

"No," Pa said. "It's called a sugar snow because a snow this time of year means that men can make more sugar. You see, this little cold spell and the snow will hold back the leafing of the trees, and that makes a longer run of sap.

"When there's a long run of sap, it means that Grandpa can make enough maple sugar to last all the year, for common every day. When he takes his furs to town, he will not need to trade for much store sugar. He will get only a little store sugar, to have on the table when company comes."

"Grandpa must be glad there's a sugar snow," Laura said.

"Yes," Pa said, "he's very glad. He's going to sugar off again next Monday, and he says we must all come."

Pa's blue eyes twinkled; he had been saving the best for the last, and he said to Ma,

"Hey, Caroline! There'll be a dance!"

Ma smiled. She looked very happy, and she laid down her

mending for a minute. "Oh, Charles!" she said.

Then she went on with her mending, but she kept on smiling. She said, "I'll wear my delaine."

Ma's delaine dress was beautiful. It was a dark green, with a pattern over it that looked like ripe strawberries. A dressmaker had made it, in the East, in the place where Ma came from when she married Pa and moved out west to the Big Woods in Wisconsin. Ma had been fashionable, before she married Pa, and a dressmaker had made her clothes.

The delaine was kept wrapped in paper and laid away. Laura and Mary had never seen Ma wear it, but she had shown it to them once. She had let them touch the beautiful dark red buttons that buttoned the basque up the front, and she had shown them how neatly the whalebones were put in the seams, inside, with hundreds of crisscross stitches.

It showed how important a dance was, if Ma was going to wear the beautiful delaine dress. Laura and Mary were excited. They bounced up and down on Pa's knees, and asked questions about the dance until at last he said,

"Now you girls run along to bed! You'll know all about the dance when you see it. I have to put a new string on my fiddle."

There were sticky fingers and sweet mouths to be washed. Then there were prayers to be said. By the time Laura and Mary were snug in their trundle bed, Pa and the fiddle were both singing, while he kept time with his foot on the floor:

> I'm Captain Jinks of the Horse Marines,
> I feed my horse on corn and beans,
> And I often go beyond my means,
> For I'm Captain Jinks of the Horse Marines,
> I'm captain in the army!

From *Little House in the Big Woods*

Victor and the Pirate

A Story of New Orleans during the War of 1812
By Ruby Lorraine Radford

VICTOR shook the wrought-iron gate of the courtyard. Mammy Bella had locked it securely before she went to market, just when he was so eager to go across the cobblestone street and read that thrilling sign again.

All day long people had been stopping to read that sign. Then with a shake of their heads they would move on down the street. Never before had such a sign been posted on the streets of New Orleans. Governor Clairborne was offering five hundred dollars' reward for the capture of the pirate, Jean Lafitte.

Clumps of hibiscus, growing along the banquette, kept Victor from feasting his eyes upon the message itself, so he found footing for his chubby feet in the elaborate design of the gate. Not until he was clinging to the spiked top did he remember that his parents had forbidden him to climb the gate. He would just stay there one minute. Scarcely had he settled himself when a flashily dressed young man came swinging around the corner.

129

VICTOR AND THE PIRATE

He paused before the sign, then drew back his head, and a merry laugh came rippling from his throat. Then to Victor's amazement he reached out and tore the paper away.

Victor could not have been more surprised. He gave one gasp of astonishment and prepared to return to the courtyard. This excitement was so great that he missed his footing and a spike of the gate top caught the sleeve of his blouse and held him fast.

Victor yelled for help! His panic grew worse on remembering that even his mother had gone to call on a friend. There was no one at home. Then he heard somebody outside the gate, shaking it. He could see nothing but the flagstones under him.

"The gate's locked!" he managed to gasp.

Then the footsteps ran along the banquette, followed by the scraping of boughs against the brick wall. Then Victor knew his rescuer was climbing into the courtyard by way of the low-hanging branches of the live oak that reached to the street.

A moment later two strong arms seized his fat, swinging legs, lifted him upward so that the torn blouse was freed from the spike, then set him down on the walk.

Victor was red-faced and breathless as he said, "Thank you!"

His eyes traveled upward the long length of the man, then he almost lost his breath again. He had been rescued by the man who had torn Governor Clairborne's sign from the post! Victor quickly covered his surprise and remembered his manners.

"Will you come up to the house, sir," said the little boy, motioning across the flower-filled courtyard, "and wait until my mother comes home?"

"I will sit down just a minute," said the handsome man, and moved to a chair by a table in the middle of the courtyard.

Victor felt he must be a fine gentleman, for he spoke so beautifully in French. He was thinking this even while he looked at the jagged rip in his silk blouse.

"Your shirt is spoiled, is it not?" said the man, kindly.

"Yes, and Mother will know I climbed to the gate top. Something always happens to me when I break Mother's rules."

"But what were you doing on the gate top?" asked the young man with a twinkle in his dark eyes.

"I climbed there to watch the people read that sign about the pirate. My father is Dr. Andre, and he says this Jean Lafitte is a big lawbreaker, and that he will surely be caught."

"So you think Jean Lafitte a big lawbreaker."

"That's what my father says, and he's a great physician who knows most everything. He says in these terrible times when we are at war that all those pirates down on Barataria Bay should help Louisiana defend herself."

Victor's round dark eyes were very serious as he repeated the words he had heard his father say so many times. The thin-faced man's eyes had grown serious, too.

"So you think Jean Lafitte a big lawbreaker. And what about yourself, my lad; are you not a lawbreaker, too?"

"That wasn't such a terrible thing, climbing to the gate top!"

"But it is against your mother's law, is it not? If you break little laws when you are little, will it not be easy to break big ones when you're big?"

Victor nodded. Then he thought of a way to defend himself. "But it's not quite as bad as being a pirate. A pirate does harm to many people. He kills people and robs their ships."

"All pirates do not kill," said the young man.

"But they do harm to others just the same," insisted the boy. "I didn't hurt anybody but myself by climbing the gate."

"Don't you think your parents would have been very sad if you had broken your neck? That might have happened if I had not come along."

"And I do thank you," Victor hastened to say again. "Won't you please let me get you a glass of fruit juice? Mammy Bella set a pitcher to cool before she went to market."

"I am thirsty," admitted the stranger, and Victor hurried into the house for the pitcher and glasses.

When the boy came out the twinkle had returned to his guest's eyes. As Victor filled the glass the stranger said, "Now I must ask one more favor of you. Will you bring me pen and a piece of paper. There is something I want to write."

While Victor sat on a bench near-by, the stranger busied himself with writing. Suddenly he arose.

"I thank you for your hospitality, young man. I am sorry I cannot wait to meet your parents. Perhaps I shall see them and you again. You have set me thinking."

He bent down and kissed the boy on his cheek. Then Victor knew he had entertained a man of his beloved France, for the kiss of greeting and parting was a custom of his country.

The stranger walked away, carrying with him the paper on which he had written. Deftly he swung to the oak limb, and climbed across it over the garden wall the way he had come.

So busy was Victor wondering about his guest that he was not rebellious when his mother punished him for disobedience by forbidding him to leave the courtyard the rest of the day.

It was early next morning before Victor was free to stroll out and cross the cobblestone street to view the spot where the governor's sign had been. By now he was sure that the stranger was some fine officer sent by the governor to remove the sign. Perhaps already the pirate had been captured.

As Victor drew near the place where the sign had been, he found a crowd of curious people. He had to go around the old Spaniard who sold gaudy wax flowers, for he wanted to read the sign himself. As he read, his heart beat faster and faster until he was certain those around him must hear it beating.

"Five thousand dollars is offered for the capture of Governor Clairborne by Jean Lafitte."

It was not only those daring words that filled the chubby boy with terror, but the message was written on the very piece of paper he had handed the stranger yesterday. Victor's head was spinning —his guest must have been the pirate, Jean Lafitte.

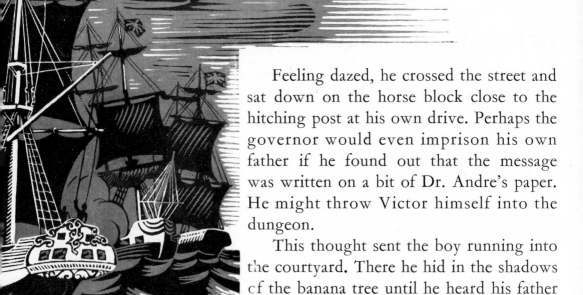

Feeling dazed, he crossed the street and sat down on the horse block close to the hitching post at his own drive. Perhaps the governor would even imprison his own father if he found out that the message was written on a bit of Dr. Andre's paper. He might throw Victor himself into the dungeon.

This thought sent the boy running into the courtyard. There he hid in the shadows of the banana tree until he heard his father drive in from seeing some sick people. Then Victor ran and confessed what had happened.

"Don't worry, son," soothed Dr. Andre. "I'll take down that sign and no one will know it was written on my paper."

When his father came into the dining room at dinner and announced he had torn up the paper, Victor found he could breathe freely for the first time in hours.

It was a long time before Victor could get over the fear he might meet the pirate again. Then, suddenly, the old Creole city was plunged into great danger. The British fleet approached the city, and every loyal person came to help defend New Orleans.

One evening Dr. Andre came in to announce that Jean Lafitte and the daring Captain Dominique had brought their men up from Barataria Bay to help General Jackson drive away the British. Victor's heart was filled with gladness that Jean Lafitte was on their side. But he did not realize that he, himself, had had something to do with the change in the pirate.

After the victory in the Battle of New Orleans, General Jackson rode forth on his fine horse to review his troops, who had fought so bravely. Not far behind him rode Dr. Andre, and mounted beside him was his son, Victor.

VICTOR AND THE PIRATE

The boy was filled with pride as they approached the line where the pirate stood. Victor's heart seemed to stop beating, for he recognized Jean Lafitte, soiled with the stains of battle.

At the same moment Lafitte saw Victor. He stepped forward. "I'm glad to see you again, my boy," he said.

Victor could find no speech in that moment of joy and excitement. He heard his father say, "I'm glad to see you, Jean Lafitte. The battle might not have been won but for you and your men."

"All this battle was not won on the field, sir," said Lafitte. "Some of it was won back in your garden. Perhaps your son has already told you about our discussion of lawbreaking."

"He certainly has." The doctor smiled.

The young soldier saluted and stepped back into the ranks. As Dr. Andre rode on, he bent close to his son's ear and whispered. "So, you see, Victor, you helped to win this battle, too."

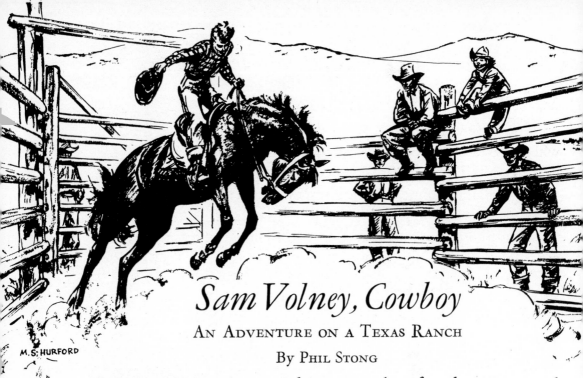

Sam Volney, Cowboy

AN ADVENTURE ON A TEXAS RANCH

By PHIL STONG

THE BIG spring round-up was only a few days away, and the stable yards and corrals were unusually full and happy.

Shorty, the foreman of the Circle V ranch, had called in all the crews off the ranges to report the locations of the cattle, and they were busy preparing for the great semi-annual event.

Sam Volney, whose father owned the ranch, was busy, too, learning to use a lariat. First, he learned the trick of throwing the rope around a fence post. Then he practiced on horseback, and finally he was so good that he could rope a post while his pony was dashing along at a gallop.

Sam's pony was named Sam, too, for Sam Houston, one of the first generals and governors of Texas. Naturally a horse named for a governor would be obliged to be smart and not disgrace the governor. He was a four-year-old that Sam had raised. Shorty had gaited him and trained him. He was a well-behaved mount, unless Sam gave him the signal to buck. Then no one but Shorty could stick to him. His gaits were so pretty that every new cowhand who came asked to try him out—once. Sam would let him prance around for a while and then he would whistle—and another cowhand would bite the dust.

SAM VOLNEY, COWBOY

The round-up time finally arrived. It is one thing to ride a horse on a straight road. It is another to wrangle cattle, one minute being crowded and jostled in the herd, and the next dashing off after some stray. So each cowhand had anywhere from six to a dozen horses, and changed every hour or so.

By the third day the older cattle had been separated, except for the mooie cows with their calves. Since there were thousands of these, there was still a great deal of work to be done. Sam rode around somewhat discontentedly, because he had been warned to keep away from the cattle. But with the departure of the main herds, no one paid much attention to seeing how close Sam got to the field of excitement.

Sam's father already had fifteen hundred head of older heifers and steers, just right to sell or too poor to be worth keeping, on their way to the shipping point seventy miles to the northeast. There was neither a road nor a fence, except those the cowhands' horses furnished as they went, by fast riding, up and down the herd. If one steer dropped out, a dozen others seemed to think he had made some great discovery and went racing after him. Then all had to be driven back again.

Back at the round-up, everyone was beginning to wish that the thing would get over. Herding the cattle was what they were used to, but riding into a crowd of sour-faced mama cows and cutting out a calf to be vaccinated with a branding iron, so that it could be identified in future round-ups, was just hard work. It wasn't like riding the range.

The horses were getting tired of being pushed and shoved around by a lot of mooie cows; and the cowboys were getting tired of steering themselves and the horses through a lot of old ladies with squalling children.

In the meantime, while everyone was too busy to notice, Sam had been riding in closer and closer. He had even shooed a number

of cattle, which were drifting away from the disturbed and excited throng, quietly back to take their turns.

The herd thinned rapidly, but there were still three or four hundred the day Shorty got into trouble. It wasn't serious trouble—he knew too much for that—but Sam thought it was. Shorty was taking a calf out of the herd and watching its mother, when a totally strange cow decided that the calf must be a nephew of hers, or a distant relative of some kind. She butted full into Shorty's horse at the shoulders.

The pony staggered and was turning clear around. Shorty bounced a bit in his saddle, which is usually a bad sign, as anyone can see at a rodeo. He straightened out his big roan, but just then there was a yell. "Hi, Sammy! Get in, boy!"

Sam's horse dashed into the crowd of cattle, shouldering and picking his way. In almost no time he was in the middle of the herd and between Shorty and the fighting heifer. Sam had the butt of his quirt ready to slap her on the nose if she made any more trouble, but by now the cow had been pushed back and had forgotten all about the business.

"Come on, Sammy, take him out!"

Shorty had his horse straightened and was starting for the

calf when Sammy and Sam slid by him. Sammy's horse began to move this way and that, crowd with his hips and shove with his shoulders, so that he chased mother and calf into the little temporary corral in no time.

Sam flung his lasso and the next minute the calf was a Circle V, bawling for its mama, after all the excitement.

One of the cowhands turned up immediately. "Who'd you say is the foreman of the Circle V?" he asked Shorty, with a grin.

Shorty turned to Sam, "Say, son, where'd you learn to cut out a critter like that?"

"I didn't have to learn. I just showed Sammy what calf I was after and he did the rest."

"Hadn't heard of you goin' to many round-ups lately."

"No. Sammy and I used to practice with the calves in the corral."

At this moment Sam's father rode up with a very stern face. "Young man, if I ever hear of you doing a trick like that again until you're big enough, I'll take that fancy quirt and use it where it belongs." He looked his son up and down severely. Then he smiled a little.

Adapted from *Cowhand Goes to Town*

139

Zebedee, Fisherman

A Story of Nova Scotia

By Alice Dalgliesh

ZEBEDEE lived in a fishing village in Nova Scotia. His home was a white house by the edge of the sea.

When he was not in school or asleep, there were two places where Zebedee could be found. One was the old white boat on the beach just below his own cottage. The other was the wharf where the fishing boats came and went. It was on the Bay of Fundy, just half a mile over the hill.

Everyone knew Zebedee because of his wide, cheerful smile and his very blue eyes. They were even bluer than the Bay of Fundy, and that is very blue indeed.

When people first met him they would say, " 'Zebedee'? What a strange name for a little boy!"

Zebedee did not mind having a strange name, because in the first place everyone called him Zeb, and in the second place his mother had explained to him exactly how he happened to have that name. This is the story:

ZEBEDEE, FISHERMAN

When Zebedee was born he was the only child in the family, so, of course, all the aunts and uncles and grandparents wanted to have something to say about his name. The aunts suggested "Earl" and "Everard" and "Leslie." The uncles suggested "John" and "Thomas" and "Richard." The baby's mother did not care for any of these, nor did the baby's father. There was so much discussion over the naming of this blue-eyed scrap of a baby that when the time came to take him to church to be baptized nothing had been decided. This was serious. The minister was waiting and there was the baby in his long, white, embroidered christening robe. What was to be done about it?

"There is only one thing we can do," said Grandfather Harris. He sat and took the family Bible on his knees. "The first name at which the Book opens shall be the child's."

Grandfather Harris put on his spectacles, opened the Bible, and ran his finger down the page. The aunts and the baby's mother held their breath, hoping the name would not be "Ezekiel" or "Methuselah." Grandfather Harris cleared his throat.

"It is a good name for a fisherman's son, for it was the name of a fisherman," he said. "The name is 'Zebedee.'"

Perhaps it was because of his name that Zebedee wished so much to be a fisherman. He loved the sea; he loved boats and fishing lines and rubber boots. He thought there was nothing in the world so interesting and exciting. It was interesting and exciting all the year round—spring, summer, and autumn.

In the spring it was lobster fishing.

All winter long there was a fence of lobster pots at one side of Zeb's house. In the spring, Zeb's father piled the lobster pots onto an oxcart and jogged slowly up to the Bay of Fundy. Zeb rode on the cart while his father walked. Up the hill they went, past Miss Letty's house, and down the steep hill to the wharf. The oxen were so strong and sure-footed they did not seem to

mind the heavy load or the rough road.

When the lobster pots were loaded on the boats, Zeb's father and the fishermen pushed off, leaving him on the wharf.

"Lobster fishing is too cold for little boys," they said.

Zeb went home slowly and sadly.

In the summer Zebedee was almost always on the wharf, but the fishermen would not take him out with them.

"Little boys are a nuisance in boats," they said.

So Zeb watched the boats go out and walked on the wharf among the piles of cod that lay drying in the sun. Sometimes the men would let him help to pile the dried fish into neat little rounded stacks, fish on fish, tail to tail.

When the fishing boats came in, Zeb thought there was nothing more exciting than to help unload the silvery cod and haddock, mackerel, and pollock. When the fish were unloaded, Zeb and his father walked home, their rubber boots all covered with glistening scales, their rubber coats smelling of fish.

On autumn evenings Zeb was sometimes allowed to stay up late and watch the fishermen drive the herring from Saint Mary's Bay into the Cove. Back and forth on the water darted the fishing boats, each with a flaming torch at the bow. The herring came straight for the flares, and soon the Cove was full of tiny fish, leaping from the water.

Zeb could scarcely stay on the wharf; he longed to have a net and scoop the herring into the boats. The fishermen would not take him out with them.

"It is dangerous for little boys when we have a torch in the boat," they said.

"It's always dangerous for little boys," said Zeb, sadly.

At last, when Zeb was seven years old, his father took him fishing. Zeb had to wake up very early. He put on two pairs of stockings, two sweaters, and over the sweaters his rubber coat. Last of all he put on his mittens, which were white, as a fisherman's mittens must be. It was quite difficult to walk up the hill to the Bay of Fundy in all those clothes. The morning was cold and it was still almost dark. Zeb began to wonder if he really wanted to be a fisherman.

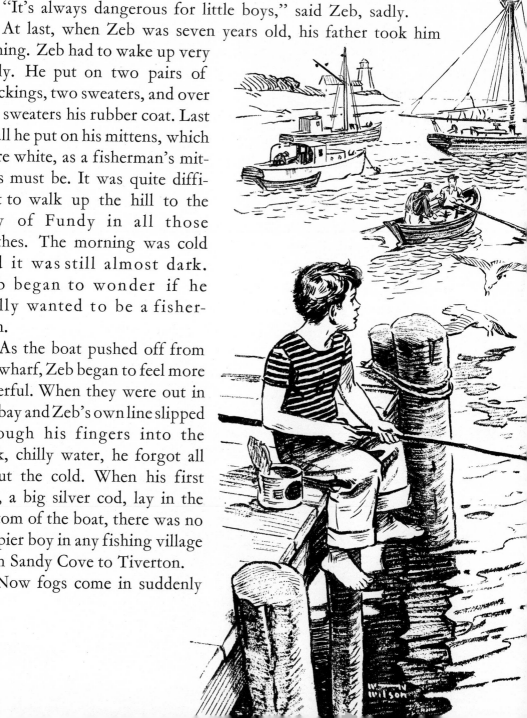

As the boat pushed off from the wharf, Zeb began to feel more cheerful. When they were out in the bay and Zeb's own line slipped through his fingers into the dark, chilly water, he forgot all about the cold. When his first fish, a big silver cod, lay in the bottom of the boat, there was no happier boy in any fishing village from Sandy Cove to Tiverton.

Now fogs come in suddenly

on Fundy, and before the fishermen knew it, a thick white fog had blotted out the land. There was no beach to be seen, no bluffs; even the wharf had vanished from sight. Perhaps they were opposite the wharf—perhaps they were nearer the wicked rocks just off the point.

They drifted, waiting for the fog to clear. The boat bobbed up and down on the water, and Zeb began to feel queer. His hands were cold, but he said nothing. He was sure it was hours before the fog lifted enough for them to see. Then the surprising thing was that they were only a few yards from the end of the wharf! How good the sturdy gray piles looked to Zeb! By the time he had climbed the ladder at the side of the wharf, and started up the hill, he began to feel better, though his head was dizzy and his legs were shaky. In his right hand Zeb carried the big silver cod, in his left hand a large pollock. His rubber boots were covered with glittering fish scales.

At the top of the hill Zeb and his father met Miss Letty's twins coming back from the village.

"Look!" said Zeb, holding up his fish. Abigail and Sara looked, and agreed that they were the finest fish that had ever come out of the Bay of Fundy.

Farther down the hill, they met Miranda Saunders with a white

kitten tucked under her arm. Miranda did not say a word, but Zeb knew that she wished she could go fishing.

When they reached the little house by the Cove, Zeb's mother was at the gate watching for him. A refreshing smell of dinner came through the front door. Zeb's mother admired the silver cod and the fine pollock.

"Weren't you afraid, out there in the fog?" she asked.

"No!" said Zebedee.

"Weren't you cold?"

"Not a bit!" said Zebedee, though his hands were blue.

"Or seasick?"

"Of course not"—although the ground on which he stood had a curious way of coming up to meet him.

There was not the least doubt that Zebedee was a fisherman!

From *Blue Teapot*

Madelon Dances

A Story of Quebec
By Ethel Calvert Phillips

IT WAS snowing. The air was filled with soft white flakes that flew about like feathers and left a silvery covering wherever they came to rest.

The great courtyard at the Château glittered like a scene from fairyland. The snow powdered the arches. It draped the balconies, and wove soft hoods for the dormer windows and the pointed roofs. Lights were blazing in every window and huge iron lanterns glowed along the wall. Sleighs, one after another, swept up to the wide entrance with a merry jingle of their bells, and in a moment or two dashed off again.

Père Coté and Madelon came walking through the snow into the courtyard. He carried his fiddle. She held a small white parcel in her mittened hand. Up the broad entrance steps he led her and in at the wide front door.

Madelon had come to Quebec on a visit, but she lived with her father in a tiny village on the Saguenay River. She was a little "habitant," as the French-Canadian country people are sometimes

MADELON DANCES

called. Her friends called her "gay Madelon." This was not strange, for she was as merry a little girl as you might meet. Her dark eyes were bright and full of fun, and she could dance gay little jigs, whirling measures. Oh, Madelon could keep step to any tune.

Within the Château, she looked eagerly about her. Brilliant lights and soft color; beautiful ladies and fine gentlemen strolling to and fro; lads dressed in plum color, with waistcoats of white, scurried here and there; all this and more she saw as she walked along holding Père Coté's hand. Madelon felt excited and happy and gay, and she held her head high.

Now Père Coté led her to the room where she was to dance, a large room, with shining floor and little tables and chairs grouped at one end.

"There, at these tables, the ladies and gentlemen will sit and refresh themselves while you dance," explained Père Coté. "See the stage, Madelon, where you will stand."

At the other end of the room, away from the tables, was a platform draped with soft curtains of velvet.

"You must dance here in the center of the stage," instructed Père Coté, "and I will stand at this side and play for you. Now we will go into this little room off the stage and I will arrange your costume and put on your cap."

From the white paper parcel which she had carried, he took a peasant dress, blue skirt, white blouse, and black velvet jacket. Madelon slipped into the costume, and Père Coté fitted the stiffly starched white cap on her dark curly head.

By this time the musicians for the dance had come into the big room and had seated themselves below the stage. They tuned their instruments and began to play a lively air.

Now the dancers drifted into the room, and soon could be heard the sound of dancing feet. Madelon could hear laughter and low voices, too, but she could see nothing. Père Coté would not

allow her to peep from behind the velvet curtains.

"You must come as a surprise," said Père Coté firmly.

The music played on and on. Then suddenly it ended with a crash! Père Coté rose and took his fiddle. Madelon slipped from her seat.

The moment had come for Madelon to dance!

Père Coté, brave in his velveteen jacket, walked out upon the stage, and Madelon followed him.

Oh, how bright and glowing the room looked now! Lights were blazing everywhere. The room was crowded with lovely ladies and fine gentlemen, sitting round the tables, all laughing and talking. The ladies were beautiful, dressed in pale pink and silver and flame color and purest white.

All this Madelon saw as she stood in the center of the stage, a smiling little habitant, her dark curls showing beneath her stiff, snowy cap, holding out her blue skirt with both hands, while she

waited for Père Coté to draw his bow across the strings.

A nod from Pere Coté and in the room, grown quiet, Madelon began to dance.

Lightly, in answer to the fiddle, Madelon danced to and fro. The fiddle sang up, the fiddle sang down, now fast, now slow, and Madelon tripped gaily in time to its song. Now she fluttered like a leaf blown by the gale, almost coming to rest on the ground, and then twirling off again when a fresh gust came. At the sad cry of the birds on her dark Northern river, she floated about with outstretched wings. Then, at the fiddle's call she turned into a merry little elf, who danced in and out among the flowers faster, faster, faster, until at last the dance ended in a great wide whirl.

The ladies and gentlemen were clapping; they were clapping very loud and very hard. Some of them were standing up. They were coming toward the stage.

Madelon looked at Père Coté. He nodded to her that all was well.

So Madelon, flushed and smiling, stood waiting. When the ladies and gentlemen reached the stage, she stepped forward and took the outstretched hands of a pretty lady in palest pink, with pale pink cheeks and golden hair and a sweet smile.

"What a beautiful dance!" said the pretty lady. "Who taught you to dance like that?"

"No one taught me. I know," answered Madelon. "But Père Coté's fiddle sometimes tells me what to do."

"Is Père Coté your father?" asked a gentleman.

And at this Madelon laughed and shook her head.

"No, no, Père Coté is my friend," said she. "My Papa is a guide in the woods and a fur trapper too. He has been away trapping for a long, long time, but he will come soon now. I look for him every day."

There were more people now, standing round the stage. They were all smiling and looking at her in the most friendly way. They enjoyed her dancing. There was no doubt about that.

"Does the little girl often dance in public?" asked a gentleman of Pere Coté.

"Indeed, no, never before," was Père Coté's answer. "There is a reason why she is here tonight."

"I will tell the reason to you," said Madelon. "It is because of Louise and of Jou-Jou, who is very ill. Louise was to sing to you tonight. It was her chance and she was very happy, for she is poor. But Jou-Jou, her little brother, fell ill. He is lame, he cannot walk. He is ill, so ill. She could not leave him. How could she? I leave it to you."

"She could not. Indeed, no," agreed the pretty lady in pink. "And so you came to dance in her place?"

"Yes," answered Madelon. "She is my friend."

The pretty lady turned and spoke softly to a friend. He turned to another friend, who nodded and then moved quietly round the room, speaking here and there as he went.

"Is the little girl to dance again?" asked the pretty lady of Père Coté.

"Once more," was his answer. "Then she must go home."

"May she not dance now, if she is rested?" asked the lady. "We should all like to see her dance again, and soon."

So back from the stage a little way stepped the ladies and gentlemen. And Madelon, shaking out her blue skirt, made ready to dance.

Père Coté raised his bow when Madelon, on tiptoe, suddenly cried out.

"Papa! Papa!" she cried, looking toward the door. "My Papa has come! Papa, quick, quick!"

With both hands she threw excited kisses toward Papa, who at last had reached Quebec from the great North Woods. When Madelon's friends had told him where she was to be found, how she was to dance alone at the great Château, Papa had hurried off in the hope that he might have a glimpse of his little girl. Now he stood in the doorway smiling, his face growing very red at Madelon's cry, while the friendly waiter, who had led him there, slipped hastily out of sight.

Papa waved his hand to Madelon and motioned for her to go on with the dance. But Madelon shook her head.

"Come, Papa," she called. "Come, clap and tap for me."

Every one had turned and was looking at Papa. They all laughed and beckoned for him to do as Madelon wished.

So Papa, growing still more red, was forced to walk forward. At the stage Madelon threw both arms about his neck and kissed him on either cheek. "Now, a chair for Papa," said Madelon.

A chair was brought by one of the laughing gentlemen. Papa, though dressed in his thick sweater and high boots, sat down upon the stage. Again Madelon took her place. Again Père Coté, his gray hair standing out like a halo, raised his bow. And to the sound

of the fiddle and the steady clapping and tapping, Madelon danced
her merriest and her best. It was such a gay little jig, with such
twinkling of feet and such bobbing of curls, that when Madelon
ended, rosy and out of breath, every one was smiling and nodding
and tapping, too.

How they clapped for Madelon! Again and again and again!
It seemed as if they would never stop.

When at last they were quiet, the pretty lady took a handkerchief from her friend, a handkerchief which held something heavy,
and which the lady now tied round the top with her own tiny handkerchief, like a cobweb, Madelon thought.

The pretty lady put the handkerchief into Madelon's hands.

"It is a present for your Louise and her little Jou-Jou," said the
lady. "It is a present of money that we have given because your
dancing pleases us and because you are her friend."

"I thank you," said Madelon gravely. "Louise will be happy."

Then Madelon turned first to Papa and then to Père Coté to
see what she should do next.

"Sing a little song, Madelon, in farewell to the kind ladies and gentlemen," suggested Père Coté. "I will play it for you."

And Madelon sang:

> "In the pale moonlight
> To thy door I run.
> Lend a pen, I pray thee,
> Till my task is done.
> Candlelight I have none,
> Burns my fire no more,
> For the love of Heaven,
> Open now thy door."

The ladies and gentlemen were delighted with the song. They clapped their hands, they fluttered their handkerchiefs like so many little birds, and they clapped again.

Madelon made a bow. She threw kisses with both her hands. She was very happy.

But now she stood alone on the stage. It was time to go. One last kiss that flew straight to the pretty lady in pink, and amid the clapping of hands and fluttering of handkerchiefs, Madelon ran off the stage into Papa's arms.

Her dance at the Château was over!

From *Gay Madelon*

In Honor of a Gaucho

A Story of Argentina

By Katherine G. Pollock

"AIEE!" Charqui Moreira exclaimed in horror.

She'd been feeling so good this morning, she had suddenly decided to do a backward somersault beside the charcoal stove in the patio. And she'd landed on top of their precious sipper, the *bombilla*.

Charqui picked up the flattened tin sipper, with the tiny sieve on the end. The sieve came apart in her hand.

"*Aiee!*" she exclaimed again, her heart beginning to pound. The sipper and the gourd were two things the family couldn't do without, no matter how poor they were. Without the sipper, they would have to do without their maté, a tea they drank daily, along with millions of other South Americans.

What would her father say? Charqui wondered anxiously. He was in their one-room home behind her, waiting to make his breakfast of tea and dry bread before going off to sell onions on the streets of Buenos Aires.

Not knowing what else to do, Charqui poured boiling water onto the powdered maté leaves in the gourd. Some water splashed the hem of her dress and dripped to her bare feet. She hopped about, hardly noticing the burning, she was so worried. Her straight black pigtail, furry-looking from sleeping on it, trembled a little as she entered the house.

IN HONOR OF A GAUCHO

"The *bombilla*?" her father demanded when Charqui handed him the steaming gourd. Without a word, Charqui took her hand from behind her back and showed the broken pieces.

"*Dios!*" Charqui's little brother, Angel, groaned in his hoarse voice.

Charqui steeled herself for what was coming. Any one of the other fathers or mothers on the patio would have handed out a quick slap, or worse, at the sight of the ruined *bombilla*. And the Moreiras were the poorest of all. Charqui knew that her father watched every penny, hoping some day to save a little so he could go look for work in the country again. He was really a Gaucho, an Argentinian cowboy, and hated the city.

But nothing happened.

Charqui felt a lump of gratitude rise in her throat. "I—I was playing and fell on it," she admitted, hanging her head.

"Well, perhaps by next week we can scrape together enough *centavos* for another."

Señor Moreira ate his piece of bread dry. Picking up the heavy ropes of onions and garlic from beside the door, he hung them over his shoulders. Without another word, he went off, in his worn soft Gaucho boots, to tramp from door to door.

"I've got to get another *bombilla*, somehow." Charqui thought fiercely.

Her father's one other meal—tonight—would be only meat, which she roasted for him on the glowing charcoal. This was what Señor Moreira had eaten when he'd herded cattle; just fresh meat. With it, he'd had his maté, quarts of it. The tea was a medicine and a tonic, as well as a food. Her father couldn't do without his maté. When Charqui remembered how kind he had been when she broke the sipper, she began to choke up.

"Yes! Go ahead, sit here and cry like a baby!" she told herself. "That's all you're good for. And breaking things."

Angry at herself now, Charqui stepped into the house and got her canvas shoes from under the bed. She undid her pigtail, combed it hard—to make it hurt—and braided it up again tight. Then out she shot, into the blazing sun of the patio, now swarming with children, and started toward the street.

"Charqui! Charqui! Where are you going?" Her brother, Angel, came puffing after her. He was so fat he was almost round.

"You stay here!" she commanded. Charqui never had to worry about Angel, no matter how long she stayed away. He'd never starve. Whenever Angel smelled something good cooking on the charcoal stoves of their neighbors, especially the minestroni soup which he loved, he'd go up to the woman and say politely, "Señora,

is there something there for a man to taste?"

It always made the women laugh to see this little round boy, who had a funny deep hoarse voice, act so dignified.

"You honor my cooking, señor," the women would laugh, and pretend to treat him like a man. But they also gave him a bowlful to taste. So Charqui never worried about leaving him.

But today she couldn't make him stay at home. Finally she told him he'd have to go back, because she was going out to earn money to buy a new *bombilla* for their father. Instead of turning back, he only grew more stubborn.

"I am the man," he wheezed,

in his deep voice. "I will earn the money." Their father was always telling Angel stories of his life as a Gaucho. Since all the Moreiras as far back as their father knew had been cowboys, Angel already thought of himself as a Gaucho, full-grown.

"All right," Charqui finally gave in. She combed his shiny black hair with her fingers, and they left the patio.

It was a blazing hot day in January. Charqui felt bad enough about herself, but she began to worry about poor Angel, who was only six. Being so fat, he began to drip. The perspiration made tracks down his dusty, bulging cheeks. But he refused to go home. Angel adored his father. He'd have trudged the streets of Buenos Aires till he dropped to get him a *bombilla*.

Every time she got a chance, Charqui went around to the back doors and asked for work. She offered to peel vegetables, to scrub, and to take care of a baby she heard howling. But everywhere, the women said, "Sorry." They didn't need any help.

Then, as they started to cross a wide street, they were nearly run over. The driver put on the brakes, and almost came down off the truck he was so mad. "Where do you think you're strolling!" he yelled at them, and gave them a good scolding.

"Si, señor," Charqui agreed politely to everything, when the man finally stopped for breath. "We were very careless."

"Si, señor," Angel repeated solemnly. The man looked hard at him. People always stared the first time they heard Angel's deep voice coming out of such a small, chubby body.

The truck driver pushed his hat forward and scratched the back of his head. Finally he grinned. "Well—here—listen. I'm on my way to the freight yards to get another load. I'll be coming back past here in about an hour. Like a ride?"

"Oh, yes!" Angel burst out eagerly.

"Is there work at the freight yards?" Charqui questioned.

"Work!" said the man. "There's nothing but work!"

"Thank you, señor. We'd love a ride. Thank you a thousand times!" Charqui told him gratefully. And, giving Angel a boost, she hopped up onto the seat beside him.

Mm! It was nice sitting down, and under a roof. Charqui slipped off her sandals and wriggled her toes. Delicious!

At the freight yards, Charqui stared in amazement at all the mixup. Trucks were racing in all directions. Men were everywhere, jumping up and down off boxcars and trucks, carrying things on their shoulders. For a minute she felt dizzy.

Their truck driver friend backed his truck up against an open freight car. And then he told Charqui and Angel they could get out and look around if they didn't go too far. He'd be ready to leave in about half an hour.

This was her chance to look for work, Charqui thought hopefully, threading her way through the trucks.

"Oh, look!" Angel croaked excitedly and pulled hard at

Charqui's hand. He had caught sight of a car where men were unloading horses. Next to his father, Angel loved horses.

"*Aiee!*" he caught his breath. Tearing his hand loose from Charqui's, he started toward a beautiful prancing chestnut that was being led down an incline from the boxcar.

The man leading the horse walked backward. He seemed afraid that he might be kicked. Angel made straight for the horse, holding his hand out as though to a friend. He did this to every cart horse, or any horse he met on the street.

"Hey, you!" one of the other workers shouted. He grabbed Angel's arm and pulled him back roughly. "Get a little closer and that beast will make mincemeat of you."

"Mincemeat out of a meat ball," one of the other men shouted. And they all began to laugh.

"Not me!" Angel said angrily. "He wouldn't hurt me! I'm a Gaucho," he announced in his deep voice.

At this all the men exploded with laughter.

"And I suppose you came along to break in a few wild horses for us?" one of the men asked, turning to Charqui.

"No, señor," she said meekly. "I—I came to get some work."

"What did I tell you! Hey, Eduardo," he shouted to the man gingerly keeping out of the way of the chestnut's flying hoofs, "don't be such a sissy. These daring cowboys will make him behave by saying 'nice pussy' to him."

"So you want a job?" one of the men, with the sleeves torn out of his shirt, demanded of Charqui. "And how much do you—" But he didn't finish. "Dios!" he exclaimed. He was so startled he jumped toward the boxcar. Everybody did.

A rearing black horse had suddenly appeared in the opening. He had a halter around his neck, with the rope hanging loose, and his dark body glistened with sweat.

A man carrying a long stick warily crept around the horse and

IN HONOR OF A GAUCHO

came hurrying down the ramp. When he got to the ground, he began shaking the stick.

At this the horse started rearing again and kicked at the opening of the boxcar with his front hoofs. The wood began to splinter, and a board broke off and fell to the ground.

"Look out! Watch him!" the man who'd been teasing Charqui shouted. "You shouldn't have hit him, Pablo. It's the Major's 'Victory.' This Victory's been treated like a baby all his life. Watch him!"

But Victory evidently had no intention of leaving the car. He dropped down on all four feet, and just stood, trembling.

While they all watched, Angel came forward and stood looking at this beautiful steed, a smile of bliss on his face.

"Look, Pablo, your life is saved!" one of the men said to the man holding the stick. "You can go home to your family all in one piece. The Gaucho will lead that fire-eater down!"

The men burst into guffaws at this. Angel didn't hear them.

"No," the man without sleeves shouted. "The she-Gaucho! She wanted a job. Here's your chance to earn a peso," he told Charqui. "A whole peso—if you lead that baby to the ground."

All eyes turned on Charqui. "A peso!" she thought. Often her father didn't earn that much in a whole day. After all, the horse had been beaten, perhaps for the first time in his life; and he was probably frightened at being in a strange place. Her father used to break horses for the saddle faster and easier than any Gaucho on Don Carlos' ranch. Half the trick, he said, was to remember that the animal was scared.

This was not an unbroken horse. He was somebody's riding horse—somebody who had been good to him. Maybe if she were careful not to scare him, he wouldn't start kicking again. But when Charqui remembered the way those vicious hoofs had splintered the side of the boxcar, she changed her mind again. She wouldn't dare!

"Afraid?" one of the men teased.

For some reason this made Charqui remember her father, how kind he'd been when she broke the *bombilla*. He was out now, tramping the blazing streets, probably faint with the heat and from having missed his heartening maté.

"All right," Charqui said boldly, and hoped they couldn't see how her knees were trembling.

For a second the men stood dumbfounded.

"You mean," one of them demanded, "you'd go up there and lead that mean-looking animal down the ramp?"

"He's not mean-looking. He's a beauty!" Charqui retorted.

Charqui's stomach felt as though it had completely fallen out, but she went forward toward the horse. "It'll be over in a minute," she told herself. "A minute . . . just a minute . . ."

"What's going on here?" a new voice broke in, loudly. "Grab that kid, quick!" it commanded.

Charqui began to run. A minute ago, she'd been afraid to lead the horse down. Now that her chance to earn that peso was slipping from her, she couldn't bear to go home empty-handed. She didn't want to watch her father eating dry bread again.

Soon the men had surrounded her, holding her back. The man with no sleeves was explaining to the newcomer, whom he called Don Jorge, that they had no intention of letting Charqui get as far as the horse. They had just been testing her nerve.

"She's got courage, that one!" one of the men said admiringly. He patted Charqui on the back, while the sleeveless one secretly slipped a paper peso into her hand.

Don Jorge was still angry. "Every time I turn my back, you cut up like a gang of children. Now, get busy!" he shouted. "Do you think—Awk!" he gulped and pointed to the box car.

There was Angel, inside the car, lovingly patting the fiery horse's face and talking to him as though he were another boy. The horse seemed as lovingly to be reaching his head down to Angel. Then while the men stood spellbound, round Angel took hold of the rope and led his new friend down the ramp.

Don Jorge came forward to take the rope himself. "Thanks,

gregory orloff

162

amigo," he said to the proud Angel. It seemed to Charqui her brother grew an inch at the man-to-man way Don Jorge called him buddy.

"It was nothing," Angel told him happily, and turned to go. "Oh—I forgot," he added, turning back. "The peso." And he held out his hand.

"What peso?" Don Jorge asked.

Charqui waved at her brother, trying to make him see the money in her hand, but Don Jorge was standing between them.

Angel was solemnly explaining that his father was a Gaucho, and that he had come out to earn money to replace the broken *bombilla*. He didn't mention that it was his sister's idea. Finally Charqui got close enough to show him the peso.

"Oh, uh—never mind," Angel told Don Jorge, and turned to leave.

But Don Jorge grinned. He took Angel and Charqui in his car to a dark little shop, and told the shuffling old man there that he wanted to see that silver *bombilla* again.

The old man was gone quite a while. Then he came back, polishing something with a rag. Finally he held up the *bombilla*, beautifully carved all down the stem and over the sieve part. It shone like the huge silver spurs their father had had to sell after they came to the city.

"This once belonged to one of the bold-est Gauchos that ever rode the pampas, "Don Jorge told Angel. "I think it only fitting that another stout-hearted Gaucho should own it." And he handed it to Angel. "With my compliments."

Angel didn't say a word. He just held the *bombilla* very carefully and grinned all over his small round face.

Silver Pesos for Carlos

A Story of Mexico

By Louise E. Baldwin

CARLOS stood on tiptoe at the fountain. It was hard work to fill the big gasoline cans his mother had scrubbed clean and shiny to hold water. He heard a click behind him and looked around.

"Pouff!" he said. "It is an American taking pictures!"

Carlos fixed upon his shoulders the wooden bar from which the two cans of water swung heavily.

"There! That's a good picture. Hold it, boy."

Carlos did not understand the words of the tall American, but he saw the camera and knew he should stand still. He thought American tourists who visited his town did strange things. But whenever they made you stand still for a picture, no matter what you might be doing, they usually slipped a copper centavo into your pocket. And Carlos had need of many centavos.

Yes, the American put a centavo into Carlos' pocket. Away the boy went as fast as the cans would let him. He staggered into the house, spilling water over the red brick floor.

"Oh, Carlos, be careful," cried his mother.

Carlos hurried out into the courtyard to add his centavo to the pennies already hidden in a deep crack of the crumbling adobe walls. Humming happily, he pulled out his penny and, without looking, thrust a hand towards the crack in the shadowy corner. His hand struck something hard. Carlos looked up, startled. The crack had been completely filled in. His father had found the secret niche where he hid not only his pennies but his drawing paper, his pencils, his crayons, and the finished pictures for the maestro (teacher).

Everything was gone! Carlos' heart stood still. Blindly he started out of the yard and down the narrow, crooked street to the plaza. Suddenly he realized that he had forgotten to meet the bus from Mexico City. Now he had missed it and the passengers were gone. Often he earned a few centavos by carrying bags to the hotels for visitors who came on the bus. Today he was too late. Everything was going wrong.

It was Saturday, market day in Taxco. Indians had come from the hills to sell red peppers, silver jewelry, toys, and all manner of things. In the crowd Carlos saw his sisters, Maria and Anita, in their best clothes. Maria wore white stockings and black strap slippers. Anita pattered softly along barefoot.

Carlos walked slowly over to them. Maria stopped at a counter of gaudy beads. Near by was a pile of shiny black strap slippers.

"Look, Carlos," sighed Anita. "If only I had pesos to buy a pair of those beautiful slippers and white stockings."

"You won't need shoes until you are as old as Maria," said Carlos.

"The foreign ladies and their little girls who come here wear shoes all the time, Carlos. I want to be dressed up, too."

Carlos laughed and wiggled his brown toes. "Shoes are stiff and squeaky,'Nita. They pinch your toes. I would not ever want a pair."

"What would you like to have best of all?" asked Anita.

Carlos suddenly winked hard to dry an unmanly wetness in his eyes. "More than anything I'd like some more drawing paper and crayons."

"You've been home?" Anita asked. Her brother nodded.

"Don't worry, Carlos. Everything's all right. I hid your things under the stone steps."

"What!" cried Carlos, not daring to believe.

"Don't shout so!" exclaimed Anita. "Father decided it was mending-wall time. Your crack he took first and found it full of your pictures. My, he was angry! He said you were not to become a wandering artist, but a respected tinsmith."

Carlos had heard his father say that before.

"Then he pointed to the pile of your things. And, oh, Carlos, he told me to burn them."

"But you didn't?"

"No. I was scared and sorry to disobey. But I remembered the space under the doorstep and hid them there. Your pennies, too."

Carlos drew a long breath of relief. "I'm hollow inside with excitement," he said. "Let's get a dulce with my penny."

They bargained with an old woman, squatting beside a tray of cakes, for a fat, sweet bun.

As they started home, Carlos ate slowly, for his thoughts were slow. He did not know how to thank Anita for saving his pennies and his crayons. Then his eyes began to shine.

"What have you thought of —a picture?" asked his sister.

"No, 'Nita, a secret." Carlos smiled happily. When he had earned enough centavos, he would buy, not more drawing paper and pencils for himself, but . . .

"What? Tell me, Carlos."

SILVER PESOS FOR CARLOS

"It's about you; so I can't tell. Wait and see."

Halfway up the street was an artist painting. It was Don Martin, who had taught Carlos how to draw his thoughts on paper. He greeted the children, and Carlos stopped to study the picture. The little terraced streets of Taxco, with their rows of houses under red tile roofs, looked beautiful. Carlos nodded dreamily. Some day he would do as fine work.

Although school was closed, the maestro still helped Carlos with his drawing. So now he said, "Carlos, tomorrow you must bring me the pictures you have made."

Carlos was troubled. "I haven't practiced much lately."

"Oh, Carlos!" Don Martin turned away in disappointed silence. But Anita could not bear to have Carlos scolded for something that was not his fault. She told the maestro that their father wished Carlos to become a tinsmith.

"But Carlos would rather be an artist like you," she added.

"Are you sure, Carlos?" asked the maestro. He did not like to think of trouble between the boy and his father. "Your father is an artist, too. He fashions fine things from tin."

"Tin is cold and silvery," said Carlos, "while pictures are warm and bright. I want to be an artist. Of that I am sure."

The maestro smiled. "We must put our heads together then, soon, you and Anita and I, and see how we can get your father to help you. So good-by for now. Adios!"

While Carlos ate his supper of tortillas served with beans and chili sauce, he said never a word. He drank cinnamon-flavored chocolate whipped to foamy sirup, and said nothing. Anita saw he was unhappy, and thought it was because he believed the maestro could not make their father change his mind.

But Carlos was thinking that he must somehow find a way to draw good pictures for Don Martin with the materials Anita had saved, and he must earn money to buy the shoes Anita so much wanted. Some day, when those two things were done, perhaps there would still be a way to buy paper and pencils and crayons with which to make still better pictures.

The next Saturday Carlos took his drawing materials and pictures from under the doorstep. He was going to make a picture just like the one Don Martin had painted, and it would please Don Martin and make him very proud. Carlos, too, would paint cream-colored houses and red tile roofs. The boy went to the spot where the maestro had sat.

Carlos sat down, crossed-legged, with his board on his knees. He began to think of Anita and how she had saved his pictures and crayons and pennies, and how very much she wanted shoes like those of the big girls and the tourist people who came to Taxco. His mind was filled with his thoughts. He thought of how Anita would look sitting on the doorstep of their home—Anita in a red dress and green apron and a blue cotton rebozo (scarf) wrapped around her head and shoulders; Anita trying on a white stocking with another stocking heaped beside a pair of very shiny black slippers with straps. In the doorway looking on stood Mother and Maria and Carlos himself. In the courtyard two chickens looked on, too, and a thin dog sniffed at the shoes. Carlos suddenly sat up in surprise. Why, he had thought his thoughts straight into a picture!

"That's very nice," said a voice in Spanish above him.

SILVER PESOS FOR CARLOS

Carlos looked up. An American lady stood beside him.

"Where did you learn to do that?" she asked.

"In school," replied Carlos.

"I teach drawing back home in the United States. I think my children would like to know what you boys and girls in Mexico are doing. Suppose you tell me."

So Carlos did. He told her about the maestro, and how he taught them how to paint their schoolroom walls. He showed her the other pictures he had finished for the maestro.

"Will you let me take your pictures to show my school children?" asked the teacher. "I'll pay you."

Carlos' eyes shone with excitement. "I give you my pictures for the American boys and girls," he said.

"Give me your name and your teacher's name and your school. Perhaps some day your class can send pictures to my class, and my class can send pictures to yours."

So she took his name and the maestro's and the school's. She put his pictures in a big book she

was carrying. As she left, she closed his hand over some large silver pesos.

"You see, this is business," she said.

The silver clinked merrily in his hand as Carlos ran down hill. As he turned a sharp corner, he ran into the maestro.

"Look!" cried Carlos. "She took my pictures to show to the boys and girls in the United States and gave me these pesos. She's going to send us pictures, and we'll send her pictures and—" Carlos drew a deep breath. Then he told how he had started out to draw a picture of Taxco, and his thoughts had drawn Anita. His face clouded.

"But, maestro, now I can't show you the picture I drew."

"You learned something better than I could teach you. Never copy another's thoughts. Follow your own. You drew a picture that lived, and so the lady stopped. Now you can buy plenty of paper with that pile of silver!"

Carlos shook his head. "Without Anita I would not have had paper for pictures to go to the United States. I am going to buy Anita white stockings and strap slippers. When school opens again, I shall have more paper. So I shall wait, for Anita will be happy and my father pleased that I do not draw."

"That is good, Carlos."

The boy ran on down to the plaza. Since it was a Saturday afternoon, Anita would probably be there.

Sure enough, there was Anita near the shoe counter. Carlos ran up to her. "Which do you like best?" he asked.

Anita pointed to a shiny black pair with jet buttons. The Indian held them out. "Try them on. They are your size."

Anita, greatly tempted, tried them on. They felt stiff and strange on her feet but, oh, they did look so fine! She started to take them off.

"Wait!" commanded Carlos, and began to bargain with the man.

SILVER PESOS FOR CARLOS

Almost before she knew it, Carlos had agreed on a price for the shoes and a pair of white stockings, too. Silver pesos rang upon the counter.

"I earned them myself, 'Nita," Carlos explained proudly, "with my pictures. I sold them."

"Oh-h, I'm glad," said Anita, as she clattered happily over the cobbles in her stiff slippers.

To their great surprise, the children found the maestro at their home.

"Look," cried Anita, twirling around to show her shoes and stockings. "Carlos bought them." She suddenly stopped and looked at Carlos. How could they explain where he got the money?

They had not thought of that. Carlos' face was pale.

"An American teacher took my pictures to show boys and girls back in the States, and she gave me some pesos for them."

Mother and Maria exclaimed proudly, the maestro began to talk very fast, and Carlos' father looked bewildered. Everyone was talking at once. Anita sat down on the floor ready to cry. What would her father do to Carlos?

The father spoke. "I am a tinsmith. So was my father and my father's father. But not even our work has gone to the United States. Perhaps I have been hasty." Here he dropped something into the maestro's hand. "I am proud of the boy. Buy him materials and help him. If I cannot make of him a good tinsmith, perhaps you can make him a good artist."

Carlos' mother beamed upon the maestro. "I am proud that my son can follow his heart and his teacher."

"Perhaps I can earn some centavos and help you, too," whispered Anita.

Carlos smiled. "Some day, when I'm really an artist, you shall have dozens of shoes for your feet—and silk stockings!"

Anita wiggled her toes within the hard leather of her shoes, and began to dream dreams.

Already Carlos was full of thoughts for a new picture,—a picture of Anita kneeling before the cement and brick stove; Anita fanning the charcoal fire with a little straw fan to keep the stew simmering; Anita with her bare, brown feet!

STORIES OF MANY LANDS

Journey to America

THE STORY OF A FAMILY FROM DALMATIA

By Clara Ingram Judson

PETAR PETROVICH hurried back from the post office, panting from the run but with his face a happy glow. "You have a letter, Mama!" he shouted. "A fat letter."

"A letter!" Mama grabbed it, clutched it to her heart. Anka, the younger sister, dropped the cabbage she was slicing. Nona, the grandmother, stopped milking the goat, and Yovan, the brother, ran from under the olive tree where he had been playing.

"Is it from Papa?" Yovan asked. Papa had gone to America nearly two years ago, in 1904, and had been trying to earn enough money to send for Mama and the children.

"From your Papa," Mama said proudly. "Wait now." She slit the envelope and spread the contents on her lap.

"It has many papers," Yovan said. This was different from the other letters. Mama read, silently. When she put the letter down, her eyes glistened.

"Your Papa says, 'Come as soon as you can. There is work for all. I have bought us a house. America is a good place.' "

"We are to go to America *now*?" Petar thought he had not heard rightly.

"You heard the letter," Mama said. "Wait, this other paper tells what I am to do."

"His brother, Josip, is to go with me to Split to see about passage. Here are tickets for Petar," Mama checked each one, "Anka, Yovan, Mama—"

"Where is Nona's?" asked Anka quickly.

Mama searched through the papers nervously and came upon a small sheet with Papa's writing. "There is not enough money for Nona this time," she read, "But when we are all working, we will send for her."

"We cannot go without Nona," Yovan said.

They looked at each other in misery. Leave Nona? She would have to go to live on the cousin's cherry farm.

"Your papa does the best he can," Mama said loyally.

But the surprise was spoiled. What would they have done without Nona while Papa was away? They couldn't leave her.

"The box under the bed," Petar shouted. "How could we forget!" He was in the house, on his knees, pulling at the chest.

"What good will that do?" Mama cried. "A few dinars! That will not take Nona to America. Don't be a simpleton, Petar!"

"Look, Mama! When have you counted these? Did you know we had so many?" Petar had yanked open the box, dumped the coins on the stone floor, where they rolled this way and that in confusion. Anka and Yovan ran to gather them while Petar began to count and set them in piles, like a banker.

Round-eyed, they watched him silently. They had not guessed

that one dinar after another, each dropped in with sacrifice, would amount to so many in two years.

"Look in the letter, Mama," Petar paused to say. "See how much it takes for one person to go to America."

Mama looked but was too excited to read; she had to turn the paper over to Petar. Not a word was spoken while he read and then continued counting.

"Not enough," he said bleakly. He looked from one to the other for suggestions.

"Stupid!" he shouted. "We shall sell the goat——"

"Sell our goat?" Yovan, the little six-year-old brother, was horrified. The goat was a member of the family.

"Yes," Petar repeated, hardening his heart. "Would you leave Nona behind? The postmaster will be glad to buy her, he is always saying we have a fine goat. The storekeeper's wife will buy the geese; she told me last week she would take them for groceries we needed. Maybe that will be enough. Or maybe we can sell something else." Petar ran an appraising eye over the room. Anka and Yovan were numb with amazement. Selling precious things— what would they do without them?

In half an hour the news had spread to the village, and friends filled the house and dooryard. Those Petrovichs, who had had such a hard time, going to America! Who would have thought? Petar had no trouble bargaining for the goat and geese, and cautious new owners took the creatures home. Neighbors bid for the loom and wheel; Josip bargained for the old bed.

The Postmaster knelt by Petar and counted out the money. "I think you will have enough for Nona's ticket, Petar," he said quietly. "Tomorrow, go with your mama to Split and get the truth about the matter."

There was little sleep in the Petrovich cottage that night. The next day, Nona, Anka, and Yovan could hardly wait until after noon when the others returned with news.

"Nona is to go!" Anka cried, seeing their happy faces.

"We sail for America on Tuesday," Petar said, "*all* of us."

"I will work hard to pay you," Nona said, when she had swallowed the lump in her throat. "And now, Yovan, stir the fire and let us eat the good food neighbors have brought."

The ship was to sail Tuesday, and this was Friday. Quilts and clothing must be washed, the house made clean. Fishhooks, bodkins, needles, and spoons must be sorted. Each person was to carry a carpetbag, slung over his shoulder. In these Mama packed small articles and clothing. Quilts were folded and tied into a bundle which was Petar's responsibility.

Sunday was like a holiday with neighbors coming and going, people visiting and saying farewells after church. Everyone made much of the children, and Petar had never felt so important.

"As soon as I get to America, I shall get a job and earn a lot of money," he said to Yovan, as they walked home.

"I shall work, too," Yovan boasted, his head quite turned with all the talk. It didn't occur to either boy that the customs, the very language, would be different in America.

Tuesday, they sailed for Genoa and there took passage in the steerage of a ship bound for New York. Yovan was frightened by the huge ship. He thought it looked higher than a church. A small red gangplank like a tongue was thrust out from a hole, and across this, a long line of passengers boarded.

The Petrovich family had a cabin to themselves, with shelflike beds on either side. Meals, served in a crowded dining room, were bread and coffee, with stew once a day. Petar and Yovan roamed the part of the ship open to steerage passengers. But the women, shy of noise, strangers, and sounds of many languages, stayed in the cabin except for meals.

On the Atlantic, storms tossed the ship and Anka was so sick

she could not leave her bed. Their clothing was too light for such weather; Yovan was kept inside. Petar turned up his collar and sat in the lee of one of the great smokestacks where the men gathered. Never had he seen so many strange people—Germans, Spaniards, French, Dutch, and Italians. Few spoke Croatian, the language of Dalmatia, and the other languages sounded like so much childish jabber. A Dalmatian from the island of Rab, going to New York on his second trip, sat by him one day and Petar exclaimed about the languages.

"You will find it a task to learn English," the man remarked.

"English?" Petar exclaimed. "My Papa is in America. In Biloxi, America. I am not going to England."

"But Americans speak English," the man said.

JOURNEY TO AMERICA

"That is funny." Petar was puzzled and doubting, even though the man said he had been in America. "Why?"

"Because it is their mother tongue."

Petar shook his head. That explained nothing to him.

"You speak Croatian, yet you do not live in Croatia."

"Everyone speaks Croatian," Petar said, "or Italian."

"Everyone you have known, maybe." The man grinned at Petar. The boy had much to learn, he knew from his own experience. "Dalmatia has been under many rulers — Turks, Venetians, French, Austrians, yet the people speak their mother tongue of Croatia. That is natural. And Americans speak English."

"Is this English hard to learn?" Petar asked. "My Papa did not write about English."

"Some find it very hard. But a man must learn it. If he does not, he will stay a greenhorn. You are only a boy; you can go to school and learn quickly."

He got up to go in, chilled with the cold, and Petar had no time to tell him that he would get a job and earn big money before he went to school.

One morning, six weeks from the day they sailed, the ship was astir early. Petar went out to investigate.

"We are coming into the harbor!" he exclaimed, running back to the cabin to tell the others. "In the night we have come to America. We must he on deck quickly, Mama!"

Soon the Petrovich family, bag and baggage, was huddled in a corner of the crowded steerage deck. Trunks, chests, bundles, and people were jammed together. Children cried with excitement and no breakfast, women looked sick and frightened with worry, while men blustered and shouted to hide their terror of this new land.

As the ship swung around, silence fell on the crowd. A gleam of sunshine lighted a statue on an island in the harbor, showing a hand raised to hold a torch blazing in welcome, a face solemn in greeting. Tears glistened on faces that suddenly put aside fear. Mothers lifted children to see the statue; people shouted, wept, cheered.

"That is the Statue of Liberty," people whispered in a dozen languages.

"This is America, the land of the free."

Adapted from *Petar's Treasure*

The Fair

A Story of Hungary

By Kate Seredy

EVER since Cousin Kate had arrived from Budapest she had been hearing about the County Fair. A whole city of tents and booths had sprung up overnight. Thousands of people thronged the alleys between the booths, buying and selling, shouting and laughing.

Kate and Jancsi, her cousin, and Jancsi's father and mother, walked up and down between the booths. Kate and Jancsi jumped and ran from one booth to another—there was so much to see! Gaily decorated whips, flutes, and bagpipes; hats, boots, shawls, blouses; jingling spurs; big white sheepskin coats with wonderful ornaments embroidered on the smooth side—all in the most brilliant colors. Farther down they came to the potters' tents. Long rows of red, blue, yellow, green dishes, cups, mugs— amusing figures, flowers, animals painted on all of them. The

woodcarvers came next—chairs, cupboards, candlesticks, picture frames, toys, candles, dolls—carved and painted and polished until every article shone like a jewel. It was a riot of color.

When they finally came to the last booth in the last row, the four of them looked as if they had been through a hurricane. Jancsi had lost his hat, Kate's black hair was all over her face, Mother's neat shawl was hanging down her back, and even Father's face had a black smudge on it. He laughed. "Can you remember what you wanted to buy?"

"I know what I want," declared Mother, wiping her hot face. "I want to sit down somewhere in the shade and have a bite to eat."

"Wisely spoken, Mother. Let's walk to the big tent."

Inside the tent it was cool and shady. Long narrow tables had been set up. People were crowded around them. When Father asked Jancsi what he wanted to eat, even the man who waited on them laughed. Because Jancsi ordered: "A big piece of chocolate cake with a pink coat, a mug of chocolate with a white hat on it,

THE FAIR

and a bottle of that green drink," pointing to the rows of soda pop on the counter.

"Bound to get a tummyache, aren't you, Son? Well, the fair comes only once a year," said his father.

While they were eating, a gypsy band came in. Grinning as only gypsies can, they started to play. They played sad tunes, lively tunes, swaying with the rhythm of their own music. People began to sing. Young men jumped up, one after the other. They threw money to the leader, ordering songs for their friends, best girls, mothers. Jancsi watched them, his face eager. "Father! Will my money buy a tune from the gypsies?"

"Just about one tune!"

"What is your song, Mother?" asked Jancsi.

"My song? Why—a czardas," said Mother.

Jancsi threw back his shoulders, hitched up his belt, and walked to the leader. He threw his silver coin on the floor, like the other men. "Play a czardas for my mother," he ordered.

Cheers and applause greeted him. "May you live long, little bantam," people cried. One old shepherd held out his hand. "Shake hands, boy. You are a true son of the plains."

Jancsi strutted back to the table. The leader followed him, playing his violin, bending close to Mother. She listened with shining eyes.

Kate tapped her heels on the floor to the rhythm of the lively czardas. "Can you dance, Jancsi?" she asked.

"Course I can dance the czardas. Want to?" He held out his hands to her. They began to dance.

The gypsies played faster and faster. Other couples joined the dance. Soon everybody was dancing, even Father and Mother. Outside the tent people stopped, then, carried away by the tempo of the czardas, joined the dance. More and more coins clinked to the gypsies' feet; faster and faster they played.

"I haven't had such a good dance since our wedding day," said Mother. "Thank you, Jancsi."

After they left, they walked toward the booths again.

"Oh, look," cried Kate. "What are those hearts?" She ran to a tent full of honeycakes. They were made in many shapes—flowers, animals, houses—but most of them were heart-shaped, with red icing. There were flowers and ornaments on them, made of many-colored candy, and little sayings written in white icing. The young men and girls give them to each other—the valentines of Hungary.

"Ooh! They are pretty!" cried Kate. "Look at this big one with the little round mirror set in it. And a saying, too!"

> You may be plain
> And sometimes even silly,
> But you are the only girl for me!

Jancsi laughed. "I'll buy it for you, Kate," he said proudly, reaching for his money. Oh! He blushed—and stole a quick glance at Father. He saw Father wink at him, and felt a coin pressed into his hand. Nobody saw it! Jancsi winked back—after all, this was something between *men*!

"Thank you, Jancsi," said Kate. "I never had anything as pretty as this! Now I want to buy something for you."

The next booth was full of pocketknives, whistles, whips, spurs. Jancsi's eyes shone. He couldn't tear himself away.

Father said, "Remember, each of you can have one gift from me—anything you want!"

"A pair of spurs," cried Kate. "May I have a pair?"

"A girl with spurs!" exclaimed Mother, shaking her head. But Kate got her spurs, the pair with the loudest jingle.

"Me, too," decided Jancsi, who was wavering between a pocketknife and spurs. He was looking at the knife, but finally he put it down with a sigh. *One* gift, Father had said.

"Mister," called Kate to the man behind the counter. "Will this money buy that knife?" She held up her silver coin.

"It'll buy two knives, little lady."

"It will? Here, give me two, exactly the same." She handed one to the bright-eyed Jancsi.

"Mother, it's your turn now," smiled Father. "And remember, nothing for the house, nothing for me or the children. This gift has to be something for yourself."

"I would like some scented soap," admitted Mother.

"Scented soap it will be then," said Father. It turned out to be a whole big box of soap, every piece a different color, and a different delicious smell. Then they bought dishes, groceries, hardware, shoes, clothes, everything they couldn't make at home, enough to last until next year. Staggering under bundles, they made their way back to the wagon.

"Are we going home now?" asked Kate.

"Not yet. Listen!" said Father.

The squeaky tones of a hand organ sounded in the distance. People were running in that direction. "The circus! The circus is here!"

"Whee!" came Kate's best tin-whistle scream. "Whee!"

Following the crowd, they came to an immense tent.

"Ladie-e-es and gentlemen!" howled the barker. "Come in and see—the seven wonders of the world! The biggest show ever! Trained seals—all kinds of freaks—the bearded lady—the man from Mars—hair-raising acrobatics—lions—tigers—elephants—trained fleas—man-eating sharks—and the miracle of miracles —the bee—uuu-tiful, girl without a body! Just a head, ladies and gentlemen—a living, talking, smiling head—and no body at all—at all! Come in and see—only ten coppers admission!"

186

From the minute the show began until the very last moment, Jancsi sat spellbound. The spangled, glittering costumes, the prancing horses dancing to tunes, the lumbering elephants with people sitting on them who must be kings because they wore such marvelous rich gowns. Then came the seals, balancing big balls on their funny stub noses, and the monkeys, so much like ugly little men. He was speechless with wonder. The antics of the clowns set him howling with laughter.

When the band played the final march, he didn't want to leave. "Come on, silly," said Kate. "We can see the side show now, with the freaks." She felt very wise and experienced. She had seen all this before with her father in Budapest.

Here were more things to astonish Jancsi. He believed every word the guide said. So did the rest of the country folk. There were gasps of astonishment and cries of surprise. There was a crowd around the glass cage with the head of a blond girl in it. She was smiling and talking. Anybody could see it was only a head. Why, one could see through the glass cage—there wasn't anything in it.

"Poor little lass, isn't she pretty—and she has no arms or legs or anything," sighed a fat peasant woman, tears rolling down her cheeks.

Kate tugged at her apron. "It's a fake," she whispered. "My father told me she is really a girl like anybody else."

"Sshh! Don't fib, Kate. You can see she hasn't any body at all, just propped up on the glass, she is," grumbled Jancsi.

"Fib! I tell you she has arms and legs. My father said she has. He said it is all done with mirrors."

"I don't believe it. The man said she hasn't, so she hasn't!" stated Jancsi. The man had a red coat and blue breeches with gold buttons and braid. He had a nice loud voice. He couldn't play tricks.

"You don't believe my father?! I'll show you!" cried Kate. She slipped out of reach and out of sight, disappearing behind the immense skirts of the women.

Jancsi looked around. He was surrounded by strange people, pressing him close to the rope that separated the glass cage from the crowd. Father was far behind other people. Jancsi couldn't talk to him. He turned to look for Kate. She was up to something—but how to find her? He cast another glance at the smiling head—the smile disappeared—the girl screamed. There was a clink of glass—the front of the glass cage fell to the ground, breaking to pieces. A murmur of amazement ran through the crowd, changing into a howl of laughter.

"Kate!" yelled Jancsi. Grinning triumphantly, the impish face of Kate appeared from behind a pair of perfectly normal legs, clad in riding breeches and boots—very evidently belonging to the poor girl without a body.

"Take her away, she's pinching me!" screamed the girl.

The guide jumped across the rope and grabbed Kate. "I'll give you a licking! I'll send you to jail!" he cried.

But the crowd was all for Kate. "Hey! Let go of that child! We'll send *you* to jail! Tricks, cheats, blackguards. We'll wreck your whole show!" They felt foolish and cheated.

"But my mirror! Who will pay for my mirror?" wailed the man.

Kate wriggled and tore herself loose from his hands. "I told you she was a fake!" she cried, slipping under the rope.

Father elbowed his way through the crowd, taking triumphant Kate and amazed Jancsi by the hand. He pulled them through the crowd, and they hurried out of the tent. Jancsi looked at him. O-o-oh! His face didn't promise anything good for Kate. He didn't say a word until they reached the wagon.

Kate was getting uneasy. "My father told me how it was done! Jancsi didn't believe it! Uncle Marton, don't be angry, please! It *was* a fake."

Father set her on the wagon. "Listen to me, now. Fake or no fake, this is going a little too far!" He held the wiggling Kate firmly by her shoulders. "You know what you deserve!"

Kate nodded, blinking back her tears. Then she reached out and touched his cheek with one finger. "But the man *lied!* It *was* a trick!" she whispered. Father scowled, but his mouth began to quiver. Kate saw it and her own face crinkled into a timid little grin. Jancsi giggled, she was so funny. Mother began to laugh.

Father tried very hard to scowl, but he burst out laughing instead. He lifted Kate off the seat and, hugging her to him for a second, set her on the ground. "You! You incredible child!" he gasped. "That man fooled me, too! Big bumpkin I am, he fooled me!"

"You won't spank me, Uncle Marton?"

THE FAIR

"N-no. Not now! I can't, when I think of your dirty little face grinning at me from that cage. You are a circus *and* a side show, but you aren't a fake —you're genuine!"

"Oh, but I'm tired," sighed Mother. "Let us go home—we have had a wonderful day."

"A wonderful day! Thank you, Father," mumbled Jancsi, curling up in the straw next to Kate. As the wagon rolled home in the moonlight, Kate, Jancsi, and Mother were fast asleep.

"A wonderful day," sighed Father. "Thank You for all Your Blessings," he whispered, looking toward the moonlit sky.

From *The Good Master*

Friend of Greece

By Josephine Blackstock

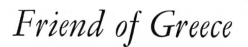

IT WAS a bright cold morning near the end of November. Nikias, the Greek boy, was leading the little black mule along the mountain trail. He was on his way to his friend, Demetrios, with food. Greece had gone to war; the enemy had invaded the country. Demetrios was a member of a Greek scouting band which went ahead of the army to gather information about the lay of the land and how far the enemy had come.

For three weeks now Nikias had been carrying Demetrios bread, cheese, garlic, and cookies which Manitza, his grandmother, had made. Papous, his grandfather, and Kyr Mihale, the schoolmaster, had trusted the boy with this important task, because he knew the hills almost as well as Demetrios himself.

Nikias had come to the slope that led to the clearing, when he heard his name called. He spun around, and there were his sister, Penelope, and his friend, Theo. Nikias frowned.

"Why did you do this, Penelope?" he said at last. "Kyr Mihale

191

and Papous will be very angry."

"Oh, Nikias," Penelope begged, "please, don't scold us. You see, the other night I—I heard Manitza and Papous talking. They thought I was asleep, but I wasn't. I heard them say you were bringing food to Demetrios."

"So you told Theo?" Nikias asked.

"She had to tell me," Theo said. "She was afraid to follow you unless I brought her."

"It was a wicked thing to do, Penelope," Nikias said. He did not know what to do. Of course, Penelope, and Theo, too, would not want any harm to come to the regiment. But what would Kyr Mihale say if he knew Penelope and Theo had followed him? What was it Demetrios had said? *Obey orders and use your head!* Suppose he let them come as far as the clearing, and then told them to go back with the black mule?

"I will let you come as far as the clearing," Nikias said. His voice did not sound as it usually did; it was just like Kyr Mihale's.

Penelope did not say anything; she was looking out the corner of her eye at Nikias. He looked stern; he did not look at all like himself. The little black mule began to pick its way carefully down the trail, and the children followed.

Presently they came to the ravine. Nikias was just easing the mule down the slope, making a little coaxing sound with his lips, when there came a tiny sharp rattle of stones. All three of them stood quite still. There was a second trail down the slope, and along it was coming a party of six men, dressed in a strange uniform. They were scrambling down one after the other and a tall man in front was waving to the children.

Nikias thought his heart had stopped beating. *He knew who those men were!* He had seen a picture of them in the paper Kyr Mihale had from Athens. They were soldiers of the enemy! He felt Penelope's fingers digging into his arm. He heard Theo's breath coming in choking sounds. *They* knew, too.

"Nikias," Theo whispered, "they—they—"

"Yes," Nikias said. It did not seem as if his lips could move; they were stiff. But Demetrios had to have that food! He, Nikias, was the messenger. He would *have* to do something.

"Hark, you," Nikias said, "if they ask us anything, we must pretend that we know nothing. We—we go on a picnic."

The man in the lead was shouting something now. He was beckoning to them to wait.

"They'll kill us," Penelope whispered.

"No," Nikias said. "Just—just leave it to me."

Now the men were beside them. They were smart in their uniforms, with braid and buttons, and they carried revolvers. The man in the lead was smiling, but it did not seem like a real smile.

"A good year to you, my lad." He spoke to Nikias in Greek.

"A—a good year to you, master," Nikias said, hoarsely.

"Your face is white; are you sick?" the man said.

"Perhaps one of their goblins has stolen his tongue." It was another soldier speaking. He had queer, angry black eyes; he was not smiling.

"I—we go on a picnic," Nikias said. "We—we eat over yonder near that stream."

"Oh, ho, a picnic," said the first man. "Maybe we can add something to that."

"Maybe we can," said the second man. His eyes did not look as if they ever blinked.

"Look—" it was the first man speaking again— "here is a package of sweetmeats. I have been saving it for just such a pretty little maid as that one there. On my soul, I even think there is enough for all three."

Penelope was not saying anything. She was pressed up close

against Nikias, her hands over her eyes. Theo was looking at the ground; he was not moving at all.

"I thank you," said Nikias, holding out his hand.

"Ho, the cockerel gets more friendly," said the second man, "but the little hen hides under her feathers. Perhaps, Benito, the children of these mountains have no tongues."

"Peace, Rafael," the first man said. "I can handle them."

"May—may the holy Virgin bless you," Nikias said. He pretended to bite into one of the sweetmeats.

"Ah, that is better," said the first man. He was smiling. "Now, will you do a small thing in return for our gift?" He was looking at Nikias. "Come, what is your name? You listen, but you do not hear. Of what are you afraid?"

"I—I am afraid of nothing," Nikias said. "The sweetmeats, they are very good."

How far away were Demetrios and the others? Were they

close? Would they come down that trail over there, and the
enemy catch them? *I have to say something,* Nikias thought!

"What would you have us do?" he said.

The first man stood curling the ends of his black mustache.

"Oh, it is nothing," he said. "We are looking for a band of
soldiers. We—we wish to give them a friendly message. On your
way here, did you see any such?"

Holy Virgin, help me, Nikias thought. What were those
words? *Obey orders, and keep your head.*

"Yes, we saw them," Nikias was speaking in a whisper you
could hardly hear. "They were not dressed as you are."

"Which way did they go?" the first man said. Suddenly his
voice was frightening; he was not smiling at all.

Nikias pointed up the path they had come.

"We met them perhaps a quarter-mile back," he said. "They
were headed toward the west."

Demetrios' hiding place was straight *east*, over the ridge.

The first man came very close. Nikias could feel his breath. His arm hurt where the man held it.

"You would not lie, cockerel?" he said.

"No," Nikias said.

The man said something to the others in a speech Nikias did not understand. Then without a word he turned toward the trail that Nikias and the others had just traveled. He began to climb, the others behind him.

Nobody spoke; they were watching the men disappear around the bend. Then Theo said, "That was a lie you told, Nikias."

"Yes," Nikias said.

"It was to save Demetrios," Penelope said. She looked whiter than the sheets at home.

"Yes," Nikias said.

"What shall we do now?" Penelope said. She was pressing still closer to Nikias.

"Nikias," Theo said, speaking in a whisper. "When they find out you lied, they will—come back."

Nikias did not say anything for a minute. Theo was right, but a queer thing was happening inside Nikias. It was as if he were listening to a story Demetrios was telling. He knew, without being told, what the end was going to be! Those soldiers would be coming back soon; they would guess that Demetrios and the others were close. The story, it had to end one way: *he must climb that mountain and warn Demetrios!*

"Theo," he said, "you and Penelope go back to the village. You know that path to the north; it branches off from the main trail. It is near the two tall balsams; you must watch for it. That way you will not meet the enemy. Tell Kyr Mihale what has happened. You must go right away, Theo."

"But what will you do?" Penelope said, staring at Nikias.

Nikias looked up the dark wall of the mountain, and he felt more afraid than he had ever felt before in his life. And then suddenly he felt angry at those soldiers who were looking for Demetrios, and he did not feel afraid at all.

"I will climb the peak to warn Demetrios," he said.

"But they'll come back after you, Nikias," Theo said.

And Nikias remembered something else.

"A regiment sends a scouting band ahead when—when it is near something," he said.

"You mean—" began Theo, and stopped.

"Our regiment must be close. Those soldiers were looking for it."

"And the enemy has a regiment, too?" Theo whispered.

He was edging along toward the trail.

"It may be close," Nikias said.

Then he started to run. He did not even wait to see Penelope and Theo go scrambling back up the trail. Nikias set his foot on the little slippery ledge that marked the beginning of the path up the mountain. He began to climb. Every now and then he stopped to look back, to catch his breath; but he could see no one coming.

Now and then he had to make a wild clutch at a bush or tree root to save himself from falling. He could feel his heart pounding; it felt as if it would come straight through his shirt. It seemed as if an hour had passed. Now he could see the top of the peak. It was not more than six feet above him. But there seemed no hold right there. He reached out toward a sharp jutting boulder; he thought he could swing himself up to it. But the rock was slippery, and besides his hands were wet with perspiration. His fingers closed about air—he heard himself scream—he felt himself fall.

It must have been a fall of perhaps eight feet; then he struck a ledge of rocky soil. It and the panniers broke his fall, but his body hit very hard. A pain like a red-hot needle went tearing along his shoulder bone. He closed his eyes and lay still. Demetrios was up there, waiting for him. And he had failed him. Demetrios, and perhaps—perhaps the regiment, too! He, Nikias, must save *Demetrios and a regiment!*

Nikias pulled himself up on his good arm. There was a firm-looking ledge just above. He could reach it if he tried hard. The pain in his left shoulder blade felt like a blazing fire. Well, but *Demetrios was waiting!* Nikias' hand closed about the rock. With an effort that seemed to wrench every inch of his body, he pulled himself up. Two feet, three feet, four! There, above his head were the scrub pine and the juniper bushes that marked the top. Nikias made a whimpering sound that was like a puppy's, and pulled himself over the top.

He lay quite still then. He felt as if he would never move again. His shoulder was a great lump of pain. Things were going dark before his eyes. He was falling asleep. But Demetrios was waiting; he must not sleep. He gave a shout, but no one answered. Suddenly Nikias remembered the call Demetrios made to the sheep. Demetrios

could hear that a quarter of a
mile away. Nikias twisted his
lips and called the sheep call.

Ten minutes later when Demetrios knelt beside him anxiously rubbing his hands, Nikias
moved. He had fainted, but he
did not know it. He thought he
had just fallen asleep. He felt as if he had been to some place a
long way away. He opened his eyes, and there was Demetrios
kneeling beside him.

"Demetrios," Nikias whispered, "the food is spoiled, but I
had to let you know—the enemy—they have a scouting band—
down below. They're looking for you. They asked us where you
were. I—I told them you had gone west. They will know I have
lied, and come back. They will—will bring their regiment around
the U trail below the pass. Demetrios, I—I—"

And then Nikias fainted again.

It was dark when Penelope and Theo reached home. Penelope
was limping and crying, but Theo was not saying anything at all.
His lips were closed tight. Only when he found Kyr Mihale at
Nikias' house did he tell his tale.

199

When Nikias opened his eyes the second time, he was lying inside a tent on an army cot. He called Demetrios' name, and a minute later Demetrios opened the canvas flap and came in.

"The regiment—is it safe, Demetrios?" asked Nikias.

"Aye, thanks to you, Nikias."

"To me?"

"Your warning reached us in time. Luckily the enemy's troops came without airplanes." Demetrios took Nikias' hand and held it in a tight clasp. "Look, lad, my colonel has told me I may let you into a great secret."

"A secret?"

"From what you told us, we knew where the enemy's men must be, and I remembered that narrow pass through which the enemy must travel. Our regiment will cross it. If they reach there in time, they will cut off the enemy's flank—attack them from the rear. It may mean a great victory, Nikias."

"Oh, Demetrios," Nikias whispered. It was all he could say.

"You and I," said Demetrios, "are soldiers of Greece; we do not talk of our deeds. I will but say to you: You are a brave lad, Nikias."

"I feel very pleasant inside me," Nikias said.

Demetrios got up. "Manitza and Papous and Penelope will be worrying about you," he said. "We are going to take you home on a stretcher. Also, the colonel bids me tell you that as brave a deed as yours does not go unrewarded."

"Unrewarded?" Nikias said, not understanding.

"He bade me find out what thing you would like best."

"What thing? But you know what it is: to ride in an airplane, and that cannot be."

A few days later when Nikias lay on a blanket in front of the fire the schoolmaster came to visit him. He brought good news. "The sixth regiment—Demetrios' regiment has driven back the

FRIEND OF GREECE

enemy! It is chasing them beyond the Albanian border!"

Then he drew out a long letter with a red seal. It was signed by the Colonel of the Sixth Regiment. The schoolmaster was smiling as he handed it to Nikias. It read:

My dear Nikias:

You have done a great, a shining deed for your country. You have saved a Greek regiment. You have shown the courage of Ulysses. It is not in my power to thank you properly. But this one thing I can give you, the thing you asked for: a ride in an airplane. On Monday fortnight a messenger in a motorcar will leave for a city on the coast. He has orders to stop for you in the village, and take you with him. I have little doubt that the good captain of the airport at the place where I shall send you will see to it that my request is granted. You see, he is my kinsman, and besides I have written him of what you did.

May you always hold the courage you showed that day. I salute you, friend of Greece!

Adapted from *Wings for Nikias*

HURFORD

Nanette Visits the Château

A STORY OF FRANCE

BY ESTHER BRANN

ABOVE the trees on the hilltop, Nanette could see the Château. The windows of the Château towers winked invitingly in the sunlight. "Come and see all the fine things behind the windows," they winked. "Come and see!"

Now a château in France was a castle . . . Nanette's Château was built of gray stone and had many high round towers, and underneath there were *dungeons*. Happily Nanette trudged along, watching the towers come nearer and nearer. The wooden shoes clatter-clapped, for they were going to the Château, too. Now Nanette began to climb the steps that led to the Château. There were many steps to be climbed—the Château was far above the stone cottage where Nanette and Grandmère lived. The tall towers reached right up into the clouds.

The great front door stared down at Nanette in an unfriendly way. The great front door never opened for little girls. Luckily it was not the only door in the Château. Nanette knew of another, a certain little side door, half-hidden in a tangled thicket of rosebushes. This was a friendly door. Nanette rapped and the friendly little door opened promptly. A little old lady in a white cap appeared. It was the Housekeeper, who looked after the Château when its owners were away. The Housekeeper and Nanette were good friends.

"Well, well! Come in, my dearie!" she greeted Nanette.

Nanette left her sabots (wooden shoes) on the doorstep and entered the Housekeeper's room in her felt sabot slippers. The little old lady was very glad to see Nanette. She bustled about cheerfully, asking questions.

"How are you, my dear? And how is your Grandmère? And have the chickens been laying well? Sit down and tell me everything!" she said, all in one breath.

So Nanette sat down primly on a low stool.

"Yes, my Grandmère is well. And I am well." said Nanette. Then she added, "And there is a spider weaving a web over your front door!"

The Housekeeper was quite shocked. What would the Master and Mistress say if they arrived unexpectedly and found the great front door barred with a spiderweb?

"Oh, dear me!" she said. "I must see to that spider right away! And I wanted to take you through the Château! Well! This time you may go alone! But don't touch anything! Remember, Nanette, you may look at *everything*, but touch *nothing*!"

With a large key, the little old lady unlocked the door leading to the Château. Then she hurried off to the great front door and the spiderweb.

So Nanette went into the Château all by herself. She knew her way about very well—she had seen it so many times before. But every time she came, it seemed more beautiful.

Nanette walked about, admiring everything, touching nothing, just as the Housekeeper had said. Her slippers of felt glided over the tiled floor noiselessly as the footsteps of a little ghost, from one room to another.

Such large rooms they were—each one of them was larger than Nanette's whole house! Such empty rooms, too! There was no one seated at the long table, there was no child in the quaint high chair. Nobody read the book lying open on the tall iron stand. Even the clock had stopped ticking.

Tap-tap-tap! Nanette started nervously. Tap-tap-tap! Somebody was tapping on the windowpane. Somebody wanted to come in. Who could it be? Slowly Nanette pattered over to the window and peeped out. Nobody was there. Perhaps it was the other window. No! Nobody was there either! That was strange! Tap-tap-tap! Somebody was surely tapping on the windowpane. Perhaps it was a *ghost*. Ghosts could tap without being seen! Perhaps a ghost was outside trying to come in! The Housekeeper had once whispered in Nanette's ear that a *ghost walked in the old Château!* Very fearfully Nanette went back to the first window. If the ghost were outside, he would have to stay outside, for *certainly* Nanette would not let him in. Tap-tap-tap! Right in Nanette's face! Oho!—It was only a branch of the fir tree, tap-tapping against the window every time a breeze blew!

The windowpanes were of colored glass—pink, blue, pale green. So when Nanette looked out, everything became pink, blue, and green. Now the trees were pink, and now they were blue, now they were green again! How funny the garden looked all pink! How funny it looked all blue! It was like wearing pink spectacles, and changing them for blue spectacles, and then changing them for pale green ones!

NANETTE VISITS THE CHÂTEAU

Now for the Upstairs! The stairway wound round and round, for it went up inside one of the round towers. This was the second floor, where the bedrooms were. The beds were not cozy cupboard beds like Nanette's. They were large flat beds, almost square, with a canopy up near the ceiling and beautiful curtains at the sides. They looked hard and uncomfortable, however, for not one had a nice, soft feather bed on top. Nanette had *several* feather beds on her own bed at home.

Nanette always rapped on the Best Bedroom door before she went in. Not that anyone was there! But you could never tell when that haughty person in stiff silks might step down from her gilt frame and say, "And what are *you* doing in *my* bedroom?" So it was just as well to rap first, politely.

The Best Bedroom was the largest and handsomest of all the bedrooms. The tiled floor was the shiniest, the bed and the chairs and the chests were the most handsomely carved. And the walls were by far the prettiest. These were picture walls. All painted with birds and flowers and cherubs. The cherubs were flying about with the birds. This curly-haired one looked so real, as real as Nanette's little baby cousin!

All this while Nanette had not touched a thing, just as the Housekeeper had said. Now she touched the cherub's pink cheek ever so lightly—just a little stroke. The cherub seemed to draw back! Nanette touched the painted wooden cherub again. This time he really did move! And with the cherub the whole panel moved back, scarcely squeaking! In place of the panel there was a tiny door! It was a *hidden door* to a *Secret Room,* the kind all old castles have!

"Ooh! I'll just peep in!" said Nanette to herself, shivering with excitement.

So she peeped in. The tiny room beyond the tiny door was empty. No, not quite! There was a box in the corner, an interest-

were so very thick that no sound could penetrate them.

Nobody came to let Nanette out. At last she stopped calling because she was tired. She leaned her head against the wall. Then all at once there was a squeak and a creak! The panel had moved at last! And there was the little door! Well, that was lucky! Nanette was just going to step through when she stopped short. For this door was not the same one. This did not lead back into the Best Bedroom. It led to a narrow stone stairway instead. And where the stairway led to, Nanette couldn't guess. Perhaps she could find a way out into the garden by following the stairway. There *must* be a way out somewhere.

Now Nanette was more careful. For this door might shut suddenly like the other, and leave her outside! She moved the wooden box into the open doorway, so that it could not shut entirely. Now, no matter *what* there was at the bottom of the steps, she could come back to the Secret Room, anyway.

Nanette stepped through the second door. The stone steps looked very uninviting. The dust lay thick, and as for cobwebs, never in all her life had she seen so many! They spread from step to step, and hung like filmy veils from the ceiling. The Housekeeper had certainly never swept this stairway. But the Housekeeper, no doubt, had never even *seen* this stairway, so how could she possibly sweep it?

Nanette started down the stairs, slowly and cautiously. The stone steps wound and wound, narrow on one side and wide on the other like an open fan. Down they went till Nanette was quite dizzy from descending in circles. Here was a tiny window, so narrow that not even Nanette could squeeze through. Down below was the garden. Nanette stopped to look out. How sunny and bright it was outdoors! How dismal and damp it was inside! She felt very shut in, and hurried down the steps fast as she could, eager to get out into the sunny garden.

Here was the bottom of the steps at last! But they did not lead into the garden at all! They had brought Nanette into the cellar—a cold, gloomy cellar of stone—a most dreadful place, where all the windows were barred with iron!

There were many little doors, but not one that opened into the garden. For these were the *dungeons,* where prisoners were kept long ago! All the doors were open, as though the prisoners had fled! Suddenly Nanette was afraid! She turned back to the winding stairway and ran up the steps as fast as though all the phantom prisoners were in pursuit. Faster and faster and faster! Up the long, winding stairway till Nanette had quite lost her breath! But here was the Secret Room again!

All breathless and frightened, Nanette beat against the paneled walls and kicked and kicked! She kicked so hard that the panel squeaked protestingly, and slid back! And this time the Best Bedroom was on the other side! In less time than it takes to tell, Nanette stepped through the door. Then the panel swung shut again, but who cared? Nanette was safe in the Best Bedroom with the painted walls. Never again would Nanette step through mysterious little doors! Never again would Nanette touch the painted cherubs in the Best Bedroom!

As soon as she had caught her breath, she found her way back to the Housekeeper's room. The Housekeeper sat by the window, knitting placidly.

"And how did you enjoy your visit to the Château today, my dear?" asked the old lady.

"Oh, well enough," answered Nanette. "And did you find the cobweb on the front door?"

"Yes, I brushed it right away! No one shall say that I permit cobwebs in *my* Château!" said the Housekeeper proudly.

And Nanette knew of a certain secret stairway that was quite covered with cobwebs, but she did not say a word!

From *Nanette of the Wooden Shoes*

The Music of the Scythes

A Story of Lithuania

By Stepas Zobarskas

WHEN Povilas came running out into the yard, it was midday. The mowers, having ceased work, were leaning against the heaps of hay and eating their lunch. The scythes, sunk in the ground, were ranged like cranes whose beaks flashed. The sharpening stones were arranged on the handles.

The boy, in shirt sleeves and bareheaded, paused on the rise of the meadow. His fair hair gleamed in the rays of the sun which burned like fire.

"Poviliuk," called his father, "perhaps you have not yet had your food? Come and have a bite with the mowers."

The boy did not feel hungry, but he was tempted to remain with the mowers. He ran skipping up to them and kissed his father. The meal finished, the men began to sharpen the scythes, and the forest resounded to the

noise of the stones on the blades. The crickets hopped on the flowers and tuned their strings. Far on the other side of the neighboring meadows, hammers tapped.

The men entered the meadow and again began to mow the grass. They went one behind the other, singing in chorus and striking all together as though invisible springs bound their movements. They bent and rose in rhythm.

Povilas devoured with his eyes each tuft cut, and noted the furrow left by the mowers as they advanced. At last he could resist no longer. He approached the mowers, with his hands behind his back, whistling. The stalks of the cut grass pricked. He went towards his father, pulled him by his blouse and said to him, "Papa, let me mow a little."

Without replying, his father continued to mow. When he had finished a row, he sharpened his scythe and began again.

"Papa," the boy called again.

The father looked at the sun, glanced at the sea of meadows still waving, and shook his head.

"No time to play with you, my boy. When you are big . . . and when there is less work."

When the other mowers approached, Povilas repeated the request, but not one gave up his scythe to him. So he left the meadow and returned to the house by a path. The noise of the scythes and the whistle of one of the mowers reached his ears.

In the evening the shepherd had brought back the flock and gone to gather apples. The father and the workmen had hung their scythes on the beam and were resting. When the women had finished milking, everyone assembled for the evening meal.

"Tomorrow is Sunday," said the father. "If you are not lazy, go to church. For Mother and me the church of Dudkiskis will do. But you young ones like big churches. And you, shepherd, will you please cut some clover for the horses?"

"Good," said the shepherd, preparing to go out.

"But not now," said the father. "Tomorrow morning, before taking out the flock. This evening you can sharpen the blade."

When everyone had gone, Povilas went to bed downstairs. He refused to go to the loft with the shepherd, saying, "I have had enough of turning and turning in the hay. The twigs stick in you everywhere. I am going to bed downstairs."

Soon everyone was plunged in sleep. Silence and shadows filled the room. The thick smell of grass entered by the window.

But Povilas did not sleep. He raised his head and looked out. The sky bent proudly to the earth, covered itself with stars, and drowned itself in the songs of the nightingales. Near the entrance to the room the shadows lying on the ground moved. In the corner a scythe gleamed in the moonlight.

"If I could mow a little," thought Povilas. "Everyone is asleep; no one will know."

He dressed himself quickly, slipped quietly out by the window and approached the outer room with the steps of a wolf. He unhooked the scythe, placed it on his shoulder, strode out of the garden and towards the clover like a grown-up mower.

The air was fresh. The clover blossoms bent by the wind seemed to sleep against each other.

THE MUSIC OF THE SCYTHES

But as he stooped to gather the clover, Povilas noted that it had not been cut. He raised the scythe and struck so strongly that the sparks flew. But it was impossible to withdraw the blade, the end of which was buried deeply in the ground. He tried to turn it to the right, to the left, forward, backward. Then, gathering all his strength, he pulled so violently that he fell backward. He picked himself up, looked, turned pale. The scythe was broken; only the handle had come.

A cold sweat ran down his back. He stood a long time as if stunned. At last he withdrew the blade, but it was notched and bent. Sad, almost crying, he returned to the house. He found some string, mended the scythe, and put it back in its place. It looked whole, but the string was too white; so he rubbed it with dirt. Now no one could see anything wrong.

He tried to sleep, but sleep would not come. What could he do? Perhaps, at dawn, go and kiss his mother's hand and tell her

THE MUSIC OF THE SCYTHES

everything. She would forgive
him and calm his father.

Povilas awoke early. The sun
had scarcely risen. The shepherd,
still half asleep, was bringing out
his flock by cracking his whip.
The sheep having passed through
the door, the shepherd took out
his flute and began to imitate the
birds. But the little singers whistled much better and drowned
with their marvelous songs the
thin sounds of the shepherd's
flute. The sun, clear and majestic,
rose proudly in the sky.

When the shepherd was far
away, Povilas jumped down from
his bed. He had remembered the
broken scythe.

"I will go and join the shepherd and tell him everything," he
thought. But hardly had he put
his foot outside when he heard
the noise of a window being
raised, and a voice called:

"Where are you running so
early? Go to bed." It was his
mother, who was already up and
preparing to light the fire.

Povilas stopped. The red
mounted to his face. His mother
tapped again at the window, so he

re-entered the house.

"Where are you going like that?" she scolded.

"I can not sleep. I was going to the shepherd," he stammered.

"You will have time to go comfortably. Come now and eat a hot pancake."

His mother soaked a pancake in melted butter and gave it to him. It was hot and good; the melted butter dripped from his fingers. His mother kissed him on both cheeks and pushed him towards the room.

"Go back to bed. I will wake you up for breakfast."

He wanted to stop, to tell her everything, but she pushed him away. "Run, little one, run to bed. We will talk later."

Povilas felt embarrassed; he did not know how to confess his fault. He undressed and plunged into bed again.

During breakfast his father sat at the table, angry. After eating some cabbage, he turned to the shepherd, and said:

"Thank you for the clover, but I don't thank you for the broken scythe."

The shepherd, startled, stopped eating and, with his eyes popping out of his head, said, "What? Me? I broke the scythe? But I don't know anything about it!"

Povilas began to perspire. He dropped his eyes and, bending over his plate, began to swallow his soup. His cheeks were burning.

"Well, who broke it if it wasn't you?" repeated his father.

"How should I know?" persisted the shepherd.

"I detest liars," cried his father, throwing a spoon on the table. "If you have done something wrong, admit it."

Povilas put down his spoon and slipped out. Now that his father had so angrily scolded the shepherd, he was afraid to admit his fault. In the hall he heard the shepherd say,

"I don't know anything about it. I do not lie!"

The sun had burned the earth like a flame. Povilas faced the sun and measured his shadow.

All morning he walked alone in the fields, watching the bees working. They dug into the hearts of thousands of flowers, sucked out nectar, covered themselves with the pollen, and thus loaded flew heavily, buzzing, to the hives.

By the meadows and the paths, Povilas went to the pastures. The shepherd was sitting on a stone and whistling sadly.

"I am furious. I have been scolded, and I am innocent," lamented the shepherd. "I cut the clover as well as I could, I hung up the scythe, and now. . . ."

"And you don't know who could have broken it?"

"I mowed the clover, I took out the flock, and until it was mealtime, I did not go near the house. How should I know?"

The shepherd took out his flute again and began to play. In clear weather the music resounded well. In such heat the birds resigned in favor of the pipes. Hidden in the trees, they remained with their heads down and rarely spread their wings. Povilas sat beside him and said, "Papa will scold and then stop. When he knows that you are not guilty. . . ."

"But no one will own up."

The boy was silent. His upper lip began to tremble. His conscience was worrying him.

His father and mother came back from church in the evening. Povilas met his parents and kissed their hands. When his mother brought out a present for him—a chocolate horse—he seized her hand and covered it with kisses.

"Mother," he stammered, "Mother dear . . ."

"What is it, my child, my little white clover?"

"Don't scold me. I broke the scythe. I wanted so much to mow. I did not think the scythe would break so easily."

"It was you!" exclaimed his mother.

His father, tapping his feet, scolded: "Why didn't you say so

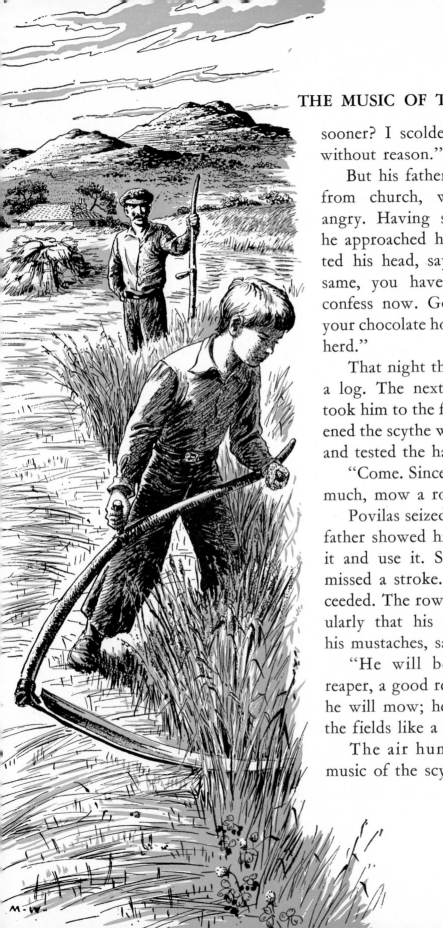

THE MUSIC OF THE SCYTHES

sooner? I scolded the shepherd without reason."

But his father, on his return from church, was no longer angry. Having scolded a little, he approached his son and patted his head, saying, "Just the same, you have done well to confess now. Go and give half your chocolate horse to the shepherd."

That night the boy slept like a log. The next day his father took him to the fields. He sharpened the scythe with a whetstone and tested the handle.

"Come. Since you want to so much, mow a row."

Povilas seized the scythe. His father showed him how to hold it and use it. Several times he missed a stroke. Finally he succeeded. The row was cut so regularly that his father, twisting his mustaches, said,

"He will become a great reaper, a good reaper. How well he will mow; he will pass over the fields like a fire!"

The air hummed with the music of the scythes.

WILLIAM NEEBE

Eggs for Sale

AN ADVENTURE IN NORTH AFRICA

By ALFRED S. CAMPBELL

HUSSEIN was watching his father's sheep as they grazed beside the winding mountain road. He squatted in the shade of a bush which gave him some protection from the hot African sun. His single garment was draped around him. The red fez he wore on his head was the only bright spot of color in the landscape, made up of brown and black mountains and distant dark-green trees. Down the valley were the tall white minarets of the holy Arab city of Constantin.

Hussein paid little attention to the sheep. They would not run away. They were hungry, and although the grass near the road was dry and sparse they nibbled it eagerly. He was watching the stream of traffic on the highway: trucks and jeeps and reconnaissance cars, speeding from far-off Casablanca and Oran and Algiers to Tunis and Bizerte.

Sometimes the trucks were filled with American soldiers. When he saw one of these, he would get up from behind the bush and salute gravely.

"Hi, there!" the soldiers would shout as the truck thundered by, and sometimes one of them would toss him a chocolate bar. The sheep never looked up; they were used to traffic.

In the distance Hussein could see his father working in the field. A camel pulled the crude plow through the rocky soil, making a shallow furrow. Behind the field was a tiny white house, his home. There his mother must be bending over the hearth, baking round flat loaves of bread for supper.

There was a clatter of hoofs on the hard pavement. A beautiful Arabian horse was cantering toward him. Its rider was sitting at ease on a saddle of red morocco leather with silver trimmings. He drew rein when Hussein stood up.

"*Labas,* greetings," said the boy gravely.

"*Hamdullah,* greetings to you," replied the rider. "The colt will soon be weaned. Do you still want to buy him?" He grinned teasingly at the boy.

Hussein looked down at his bare feet in the dust. Weeks ago he had seen the tiny, snow-white colt and had fallen in love with it. When the owner told him he was going to sell it, he had said, trembling with his own daring, "Perhaps I will buy it." He knew that it would take far more money than his father could possibly spare, even if his father would give any help at all. But he had hoped that somehow he would be able to get the money in time.

EGGS FOR SALE

Now he squirmed in embarrassment.

He looked up at the rider. "Yes, I still wish to buy him. I have not all the money yet, but I will soon have more. Promise not to sell him to anyone else until you give me a chance!" The man nodded, laughed as if at a joke, and cantered on. Hussein squatted down again to think.

The only money he could earn was by selling eggs to the American soldiers who passed on the highway. Eggs were very scarce in North Africa. The soldiers would pay six francs, twelve cents, for one fresh egg. Hussein had three hens of his own; nearly every day there was an egg or two to sell. Six or twelve francs a day; it would take a long while to save five hundred francs, the price of the colt. Meanwhile, the owner might get a better offer and sell him to someone else. So far Hussein had only ninety francs.

A truck was coming, slowing down as it approached. Hussein reached into the bush and drew out two white eggs. Standing up, he held them high, one in each hand. The truck stopped, and the two drivers got out and stretched.

"*Oeufs?* Eggs?" called Hussein. "Onlee seex francs egg."

One of the Americans looked at him. "Hey, Joe," he said, "want some eggs?" They both came over and examined them.

"They look clean," said Joe. "Sure, son, we'll take both of them. Hope they're fresh!"

"*Oui vraiment frais,* yes, really fresh," said Hussein eagerly. They gave him twelve francs between them, in small coins. Then

Joe reached behind the seat of the truck and pulled out a choco-late bar.

"Here you are, son. Souvenir."

Hussein clutched it eagerly. *"Merci bien,"* he said. "Tank you veddy mooch."

After they had climbed back into the truck and driven off, Hussein noticed something lying in the road, a flat case of black leather. He picked it up and looked inside. There were cards with writing on, and tucked neatly into a flap he saw many, many hundred-franc notes—more than he could count.

He looked around. No one was in sight except his father, plowing in the distance. Why, there must be enough money here

to buy the colt and to spare! His heart beat fast with excitement. Then the smile left his face. He was thinking.

This wasn't his money. It belonged to the American soldiers. They had been kind to him, given him chocolate. If he kept their money he would be steal-ing,—and stealing from friends who had been generous. He blushed for shame. But how could he get the money back to them? He couldn't even remem-ber what they looked like. All American soldiers looked about the same to him. And they would probably never come back.

Again he was tempted to keep the money. If they didn't come

back, they wouldn't remember where they had lost it. No one could blame him for not returning the wallet when he didn't know where to return it. The sun was very hot; he squatted down behind the bush again and thought and thought.

Suddenly an idea came into his head. He watched the road to see what was coming. First three trucks, then a wood-burning bus, trailing clouds of smoke; two more trucks, and finally a jeep with a flag tied to its windshield. He jumped up and ran into the road, waving his arms. The jeep screamed to a stop. The driver, a sergeant, glared at him. But Hussein stepped up to the officer who was riding beside the driver. He held up the wallet. "Monnee, I find," he said, and then stopped because he couldn't think of any more English words.

The officer took the wallet and looked inside. "Whew," he whistled. "A young fortune! And this kid didn't try to keep it! Let's see if there's an identification card here; yes, PFC Joseph

Robinson. Why, Joe's one of the boys in my outfit. I'll take it along and give it to him tonight."

He pointed down the road, in the direction the truck had taken. "I give money to soldier, compris?"

Hussein didn't quite understand, but he could see that the officer was going to get the money back to its owner.

"Where do you live?" asked the officer, pulling out a notebook. Hussein pointed towards the distant house.

"Name?"

"Hussein."

The officer wrote on two pages, tore out one and handed it to him. "That's a receipt. You don't know what that means, but hang on to it anyway. Okay, sergeant, let's get rolling. *Au revoir,* Hussein." They drove off.

The sheep had wandered down the road, and Hussein had to run to catch up with them before they tried to cross the highway. At six or twelve francs a day, how long would it take to save five hundred francs? Probably years, and then the colt would be sold to someone else. Well, he still had the chocolate bar. He nibbled it while watching the sheep.

Several days later the dealer stopped in passing and told him he could wait only two more days for the money. Otherwise, he would have to accept an offer from a man in Setif, who was anxious to buy the colt. Hussein said nothing, but in his heart he knew that he couldn't possibly get the money in two days. The hens were laying well, but he had only a hundred and thirty-eight francs, not half enough.

He was sitting by the roadside on the last day, the sheep scattered up and down the highway, when a car coming from the opposite direction stopped.

"Hussein," called a voice.

He started up and looked. It was a jeep. In it were the same sergeant and the same officer whom he had halted to give up the wallet.

The officer climbed out. "Joe says to thank you," he said, holding out an envelope, "and he sends you this."

Hussein took it hesitantly and peered inside. Several crisp one-hundred-franc notes!

The officer pointed at him. "For you," he smiled, "with thanks." Then he removed a shining gold insignia from his collar. It said: "U. S."

He pinned it to Hussein's garment. "You're a good boy," he said, and climbed back into the car.

Hussein clutched the money in his hand. He pulled out his wallet and counted his coins. He had enough, between the two hoards, to pay the dealer. He looked up the road. The dealer was coming toward him on his fine horse. At the end of a rope the white colt followed, his eyes bright, his little hobby-horse tail switching from side to side.

The dealer stopped. "Well, have you the money? Otherwise, I am taking him to Setif." He smiled as if at some secret joke. The boy realized that the man had never taken the matter seriously.

Hussein held out the money, while the man looked at it in astonishment. He hesitated, then shrugged.

"Well, since you have it, take him." He handed Hussein the end of the rope, pouched the money, and cantered off.

225

The Brothers One, Two, and Three

A NEW YEAR ADVENTURE IN CHINA

By DOROTHY ROWE

THERE were once three Chinese brothers, named One, Two, and Three. One was the oldest and Three was the little brother, while Two came in between. Sometimes people would look at them and ask if they were all the same age. But their mother would laugh as she replied, "No, indeed, they are eleven and ten and nine years old, so we named them One, Two, and Three."

It was the most magic time of all the year, New Year's Eve, and the boys went to bed that night whispering sleepily about the surprise that was sure to come in the morning.

One said, "I think if we could have lanterns as fine as those great green frogs we had last year, that would be best."

Two said, "I always wish for a rabbit lantern of the kind we had two years ago. Those fine red eyes, and the way their ears moved—I can never forget."

But little Three said, "I don't want a lantern like any we ever saw before. I want a new kind, a surprise kind."

THE BROTHERS ONE, TWO, AND THREE

On New Year's Day Uncle came after breakfast, and he and Father took the three boys to the toy market. The streets were full of merry people, dressed in their best clothes. Everyone laughed and wished "ten thousand long years" to his friends. And what toys! Uncle said each boy was to choose the toy he wanted most. That wasn't easy, with such trays full of exciting things.

Finally, among the stalls of toys, they came upon a man who was showing a crowd of boys how to make a bamboo top sing. These tops, called "diabolos," did not spin on the floor but were shaped like dumbbells and spun on a piece of string wound about the center. The trick was to start the top swinging and then to move the two sticks that were tied to the ends of the string faster and faster until a little whistle began to sound in the top. *"Wing, wing, ah-wing,"* whined the top, as the man moved his arms faster and faster.

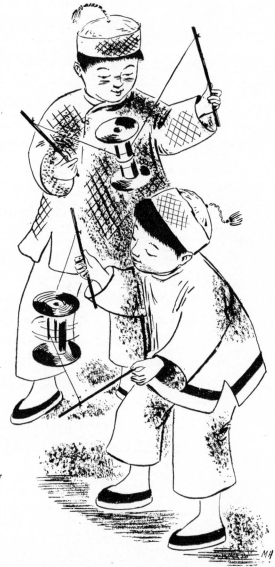

"I want that top!" said One suddenly.

"So do I!" said Two, deciding that he liked this toy.

Three said nothing at all, for he was not sure that he could make a top sing.

The man who was selling the tops said, "Would you care to try spinning it?" And he looked right at One.

"I would, and so would my brother, Two," said he, and the man took two new diabolos and two sets of sticks and strings. He showed the boys how to hold them near the ground, moving the sticks faster and faster until the tops swung humming into the air. The boys worked hard. First one arm up and then the other, and they managed to keep the tops on the strings, but not even a hum of sound came.

One and Two wanted so much to succeed. They grew hot with trying, and the perspiration rolled down from their heads under their New Year coat collars.

"I don't care for a top, Uncle," explained Three, as Uncle paid for the two tops the older boys had chosen.

"All right, Three, let's go on to some other stall."

A little farther down the street they saw a man who was dancing on one leg, his other leg tucked up behind him. With his free leg he was kicking into the air a bit of cloth with three cock's feathers sewed to it. The cloth was weighted with three pennies, so it always landed right side up, but the man never let it touch the ground. He would kick it into the air and then kick again when it came down. Over and over he did not miss, and the crowd cheered. Three heard the man counting in a low voice, and he heard him say, *"Wu-shih-i."*

"Uncle," he called, "has he really kicked that fifty-one times without stopping?"

The man heard him, and caught the shuttlecock in his hand as he said, "You are right. I kicked it fifty-one times without letting it drop, and I have done it a hundred times. Would you care to have your uncle buy this toy for you?"

Three decided at once that this was the toy he wanted. He had played "hop-the-squares" so often that he knew he could easily play this game on one foot. Uncle selected one from the large tray of them that waved their feathers in the sunlight. Three said,

THE BROTHERS ONE, TWO, AND THREE

"That one with two red feathers and one black one is the very one I was wanting."

So the great question of the New Year toys was settled, and Three went back to find that his brothers had learned to make a little hum come from their tops. So they all went home and played in the courtyard of their home.

Three, being the littlest, was the first to get tired playing. He found he could kick the shuttlecock ten times without stopping. When he stopped, Father and Uncle tucked up their long coats and kicked the shuttlecock, too. They laughed loudly and took turns playing until they had counted one hundred kicks. Then Three gave a scream of joy and they let the shuttlecock flutter to the ground. One and Two came running to see what was happening.

"Come right in at once," Three said in a loud voice. "Mother has the lantern for this year put out on the table and ready. Oh, it's the most wonderful kind you ever saw."

On the big table, there was a huge lantern. It was shaped like a great blue dragon, five feet long, with a head that lifted into the air, and green fur on the chin for whiskers. The tail of the dragon was white and forked, so it looked very real, and Two touched it to be sure

229

that it was only paper.

Mother explained about the dragon, "Here in the mouth is the place to put the candle. The body of paper is hollow, so the light reaches back and makes it all shine. Here is a round paper ball with a place for a candle, too."

"What is it for, Mother?" asked One.

"For you, One, my eldest son. You know that the dragon likes the sun, so this is a play sun for our paper dragon. Hold this stick with the ball on it. There, see how the sun hangs on that bar and how it will shine when it is lit. You carry the sun before the dragon. Two and Three carry the dragon so."

Mother fitted a stick to hold the head of the dragon and put that in Two's hands. Then she fitted a stick to the tail and Three held that. In a minute they had lifted the dragon from the table,

and One stepped in front. They marched around, keeping step
all the way, until Father said,

"By the time we have the candles lit it will be dark enough
to take your lantern to the street and parade with it."

The boys stood still and Mother adjusted the candle in the
paper sun and another in the dragon's head. Father lighted them
carefully.

Uncle pretended he was a band and clapped his hands as he
sang out, "One, two, one, two, forward march," while the boys
walked across the courtyard and through the front gate out to
the street.

Lanterns of every kind were shining in the street, but no
other boys had a dragon lantern. And no boys were so proud and
happy as the little brothers, One, Two, and Three.

From *Traveling Shops*

Ghost of the Lagoon

By Armstrong Sperry

MAKO lay stretched at full length on the *pandanus* mats, listening to the drone of Grandfather's voice. Overhead, the dark sky glistened with stars. From far off came the muffled thunder of the surf on the reef.

Now the old man was speaking of Tupa—the ghost of the lagoon. Ever since the boy could remember, he had heard tales of the dreaded monster. Fishermen, returning from the reef at midnight, spoke of the "ghost" with bated breath.

Tupa appeared to regard the lagoon of Bora Bora as his special domain. Not many people had actually seen the ghost of the lagoon. Grandfather was one of the few who had.

"What does he really look like, Grandfather?" the boy asked, for probably the hundredth time.

"*Aià!*" The old man shook his head. "Tupa lives on the floor of the sea, in the great caverns of the reef. He is longer than this house. There is a sail on his back, not large, but terrible to see, for it burns with a white fire. Once, when I was fishing beyond the reef at night, I saw him come right up under another canoe..."

"What happened then?" Mako asked breathlessly.

The old man's voice dropped to a whisper of awe. "Tupa dragged the canoe right under the water. The three fishermen who were in it were never seen again. Fine swimmers they were, too. No!" Grandfather shook his head. "It is bad fortune even to speak of Tupa. There is evil in his very name."

"But King Opu Nui has offered a reward for his capture," the boy persisted.

The old man snorted. "Thirty acres of coconut land, and a sailing canoe. But who ever heard of laying hands on a ghost?"

Mako's eyes glistened. "*Auê!* Thirty acres of land, and a sailing canoe . . . How I should love to win that reward!"

Mako's mother scolded her son for such foolish talk. "Be quiet now, son, and go to sleep. Grandfather has told you that it is ill fortune to speak of Tupa. Alas, how well we have learned that lesson! Your father—" The woman stopped.

"What of my father?" the boy asked quickly.

"Tell him, Grandfather," the woman whispered.

"Your father," he explained gently, "was one of the three fishermen in the canoe that Tupa destroyed."

Mako shivered. He brushed back the hair from his damp forehead. Then he squared his shoulders. "I shall avenge my father," he cried fiercely. "I shall slay Tupa—see, with these hands—and win the king's reward!"

"Hush!" his mother commanded. "Be quiet, I tell you. Go to sleep now. Enough of such foolish talk."

So Mako lay down again upon the mats. He rolled over on his side and closed his eyes. But sleep was long in coming.

Bora Bora, where Mako lived, is far away in the South Pacific. It is not a large island; you can paddle around it in a single day. But it rises straight up out of the sea, very high into the air.

Mako had been born on the edge of the sea, and most of his waking hours were spent in the waters of the lagoon. He was clever with his hands: he had made a harpoon that was tipped with a five-pronged spearhead of iron. He had made a canoe out of a *tamanu* tree. It wasn't a big canoe—only a little longer than his own height. But there was an outrigger (a sort of balancing pole) fastened to one side to keep the canoe from capsizing.

The canoe was just large enough to hold Mako and his dog. They were great companions, these two. The dog, whose name was Afa, was all white except for a black spot over each eye—which made his eyes look like question marks.

The boy was slow to waken that morning. The ghostly shape of Tupa had played through his dreams, making him restless. And so the sun was almost noon high before Mako sat upright on the mats. He roused Afa, and together the boy and the dog ran down to the lagoon for their morning splash. When they returned, Mako's mother had food ready and waiting.

"These are the last bananas," the woman told him. "What an appetite you have, son! I wish that this afternoon you would paddle out to the *motu* and fetch back a new bunch."

"*E pai!*" the boy assented eagerly. The motu was an islet on the outer reef, half a mile from shore. It was one of Mako's favorite playgrounds. Bananas and oranges grew there in abundance.

"Come, Afa!" he called, gulping the last mouthful. He picked up his long-bladed knife for cutting bananas, seized his spear. Then he was dashing across the white sand, where his canoe was drawn up. The boy shoved the canoe into the water and climbed aboard. Then, picking up his paddle, he thrust it vigorously into the water. The canoe shot ahead. So clear was the water that Mako could see the coral gardens forty feet below him, growing in the sand.

And the boy thought suddenly of Tupa—ghost of the lagoon. On such a bright day it was hard to believe in ghosts of any sort. Perhaps ghosts were only old men's stories anyway!

Mako's eye came to rest upon his spear—the spear that he had made with his own hands—the spear that was as straight and true as an arrow. Could a ghost be slain with a spear? Some night,

when all the village was sleeping, Mako swore to himself that he would find out! He would paddle out to the reef and challenge Tupa! Perhaps tonight. Why not? His breath caught at his daring. His hands tensed on the paddle.

As the canoe drew closer to the motu, the boy saw the white coral—a long slim shape that rose slightly above the surface of the water, a few yards from shore. It looked very much like a shark. There was even a triangular bump on the back that the boy could pretend was a dorsal fin. Up near the head, just where the jaws sloped backward, were two dark holes that looked like eyes! Times without number the boy had practiced spearing this imaginary shark, aiming always for the most vulnerable spot. So true and straight had his aim become that the spear would pass right into the dark holes without even scraping the sides of the coral. No other boy in Bora Bora could match him in skill. He had nicknamed the coral formation "Tupa."

This morning, as he paddled past it, he shook his fist and

235

shouted, "Ho, Mister Tupa! Just wait till I have got my bananas. When I come back I'll make short work of you!"

The bow of the canoe scraped the sand with a dull, crunching sound. Mako climbed into the shallows, waded ashore, and pulled his canoe up on the beach. Then, picking up his knife, he followed Afa into the jungle. Here the light was so dense and green that the boy felt as if he were moving under water. Ferns grew higher than his head. The branches of the trees interlaced to form a roof, a green roof powdered with starry blossoms. A flock of parakeets fled on swift wings. Somewhere a wild pig crashed through the undergrowth, while Afa dashed away in pursuit. Mako paused anxiously. He had no desire to meet the wild *puaa*, armed only with his banana knife . . . But the pig, it seemed, had no desire to meet him, either. Then ahead of him the boy saw the broad green blades of a banana tree; a bunch of bananas, golden ripe, was growing out of the top.

"I wonder," he mused, "why bananas always grow upside down. Doesn't seem to make much sense!"

At the base of the tree he made a nest of soft leaves for the bunch to fall upon. In this way the fruit wouldn't be crushed. Then with a swift slash of his blade, he severed the stem. The bananas fell to the earth with a dull thud. Two more bunches he found.

"I might as well get some oranges while I'm here," the boy decided, just as if there were someone there to hear him.

And so it was that he set about fashioning a net out of palm fronds to carry the oranges. As he worked, his swift fingers plying in and out among the strong green fronds, he could hear Afa's excited barks off in the jungle. That was just like Afa—always barking at something: a bird, a fish, a wild pig. Really, that dog was no use at all, Mako told himself. But he grinned indulgently at the thought. No boy ever had a finer companion!

The palm net took longer to make than Mako realized; and by the time it was finished, the sun had set. There is no afterglow in the islands of the tropics. Night closes down swiftly. The jungle became a place of gloom, but now the net was full of oranges and Mako was ready to return home.

He carried his booty down to the shore and loaded it into the canoe. Then he whistled to Afa. The dog came bounding out of the bush, wagging his tail as if he were greatly pleased with his own exploits. The little dog leaped into the bow and Mako sprang aboard.

Mako dug his paddle into the water; the canoe leaped ahead. The dark water was alive with phosphorus. The bow of the canoe seemed to slice through a pale liquid fire; each dip of the paddle trailed streamers of glowing gleams. As the canoe approached the coral formation, the coral shark gleamed palely.

And then, suddenly, Mako's breath caught in his throat. Just beyond the triangular fin of the coral Tupa, there was another fin. A huge one. It had never been there before. And—could he believe his eyes—*it was moving!*

Involuntarily the boy halted. His gaze caught and held, spellbound. Then Afa began to bark furiously. The great white fin, shaped like a small sail, glowed with phosphorescent light. It was circling slowly around the canoe . . . And then Mako knew. Here was Tupa—the real Tupa—ghost of the lagoon!

His knees felt weak. The grip of his fingers turned to water. He tried to cry out, but his voice died in his throat. Now the great shark was circling slowly. With each circle, it moved closer and closer in upon the canoe. There was nothing hurried in its movement. Tupa had all the time in the world. Now the boy could see the phosphorescent gleam of the great shark's sides; and, as it moved closer, he saw the yellow baleful eyes, the gill-slits in its throat.

Afa was beside himself. He leaped from one side of the canoe to the other. Mako leaned forward to grab the dog, but his shift in weight tipped the canoe. In another second he would be overboard. The boy threw his weight into the balance. The canoe righted. But with a loud splash Afa fell into the dark water.

Mako stared at him in consternation. The little dog seemed suddenly confused. Instead of swimming back toward the canoe, he headed for the distant shore. And there was the great white shark—scarce a canoe-length away. Tupa had spotted his prey.

"Afa! Afa! Come quickly!" Mako shouted, anguish in his heart.

The little dog swung back toward the canoe. His question-mark eyes popped in his head. Would he make it? Mako strained forward. No—no . . . Afa was too late . . . Swiftly the boy seized his spear. He sprang upright, bracing himself against the mid-thwart. There was no weakness in him now. There was only this terrible reality: his dog in peril of instant death.

Afa was swimming desperately to regain the canoe. The white shark had paused in his circling, gathering speed for the final rush. Mako raised his arm, took aim . . . In that instant came the charge. Quick as light's own speed, Mako's arm flashed forward —all his strength behind the thrust. The spear drove straight and true. Mad with pain, Tupa whipped about. The water lashed with fury. The canoe rocked violently. Mako struggled to keep his balance. Quickly he drew back the spear by the cord attached to his wrist.

He bent over to seize Afa and drag him aboard. Then he straightened, not a moment too soon. Once again the shark charged. Once again Mako hurled his weapon. The spear found its second mark. Blinded now, weak from loss of blood, Tupa rolled to the surface, turned slightly on his side. Was he dead?

Mako knew how clever sharks could be. Scarcely daring to breathe, he paddled silently toward the still body. Now Mako saw the faintest quiver of the great tail. The shark was reviving. The boy knew that one flip of that thrashing tail could shatter the small canoe, send him and Afa into the water, where Tupa could smell them out and destroy them. Mako's strength was almost gone. His breath was coming now in gasps. He thought for an instant of his father—of the vow he'd sworn. A new strength came to him. Swiftly, yet calmly, he stood upright, braced himself firmly. Then, uttering a silent prayer to the Shark God, he hurled his spear for the last time. It was now or never. Downward, swift as sound, the spear plunged into a white shoulder...

Peering over the side of the canoe, Mako could see the great fish turn over far below the surface. A luminous mist clouded the black water. Then slowly, slowly, the great shark rose to the surface of the lagoon. There he floated, half on one side.

Tupa was dead.

Mako flung back his head and shouted for joy. Then, hitching a stout line about the shark's tail, the boy began to paddle back toward shore. The dorsal fin, like a small triangular sail, burned with the white fire of phosphorus, trailing after the canoe.

Men were running down to the beaches of Bora Bora, shouting as they leaped into their canoes and put out across the lagoon. Their cries reached the boy across the water.

"*Auē te auē!* It is Tupa—ghost of the lagoon. Mako has killed him!"

That night, as the weary boy lay on the mats listening to the distant thunder of the sea, he heard Grandfather inventing a new song, the song which would be sung on the morrow at the feast which King Opu Nui would give in Mako's honor. The boy saw his mother bending over the cook-fire, stirring a fragrant broth. The stars leaned close, winking like friendly eyes. Grandfather's voice reached him now from a great distance: "Thirty acres of land, and a sailing canoe . . ."

All was right with the world. Mako was asleep and dreaming.